REA

ALLEN COUNTY PUBLIC LIBRARY

3 ♡ **P9-BHR-225**

"Are You Sure You Want To Go Through With This, Katie?" Neil Heard His Mother Ask. "You Know What It Means...."

"It means my baby will be illegitimate," Katie replied simply.

Neil noted the pain on her face. He was very disappointed in how his parents were taking the news.

"Don't you see?" Richard demanded. "We're trying to salvage what's left of her reputation."

Neil cut in. "Okay, the two of you have said enough." His parents stared at him. "Katie has a *fine* reputation. Her only mistake was falling for the wrong guy." He turned to Katie, and his heart wrenched at the sight of her glistening eyes. "You want a name for your baby, you got it. I'll give you mine."

"Neil, what are you saying?" his mother asked.

His gaze never left Katie's. "That should be obvious," he said. "I'm asking Katie to marry me."

ROMANCE

Dear Reader,

Dog days of summer got you down? Chill out and relax with six brand-new love stories from Silhouette Desire!

August's MAN OF THE MONTH is the first book in the exciting family-based saga BECKETT'S FORTUNE by Dixie Browning. *Beckett's Cinderella* features a hero honor-bound to repay a generations-old debt and a poor-but-proud heroine leery of love and money she can't believe is offered unconditionally. *His E-Mail Order Wife* by Kristi Gold, in which matchmaking relatives use the Internet to find a high-powered exec a bride, is the latest title in the powerful DYNASTIES: THE CONNELLYS series.

A daughter seeking revenge discovers love instead in *Falling for the Enemy* by Shawna Delacorte. Then, in *Millionaire Cop & Mom-To-Be* by Charlotte Hughes, a jilted, pregnant bride is rescued by her childhood sweetheart.

Passion flares between a family-minded rancher and a marriage-shy divorcée in Kathie DeNosky's *Cowboy Boss*. And a pretend marriage leads to undeniable passion in *Desperado Dad* by Linda Conrad.

So find some shade, grab a cold one…and read all six passionate, powerful and provocative new love stories from Silhouette Desire this month.

Enjoy!

Joan Marlow Golan

Joan Marlow Golan
Senior Editor, Silhouette Desire

Please address questions and book requests to:
Silhouette Reader Service
U.S.: 3010 Walden Ave., P.O. Box 1325, Buffalo, NY 14269
Canadian: P.O. Box 609, Fort Erie, Ont. L2A 5X3

Millionaire Cop
& Mom-To-Be
CHARLOTTE HUGHES

Silhouette
Desire

Published by Silhouette Books
America's Publisher of Contemporary Romance

If you purchased this book without a cover you should be aware that this book is stolen property. It was reported as "unsold and destroyed" to the publisher, and neither the author nor the publisher has received any payment for this "stripped book."

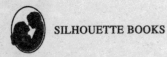

SILHOUETTE BOOKS

ISBN 0-373-76456-1

MILLIONAIRE COP & MOM-TO-BE

Copyright © 2002 by Charlotte Hughes

All rights reserved. Except for use in any review, the reproduction or utilization of this work in whole or in part in any form by any electronic, mechanical or other means, now known or hereafter invented, including xerography, photocopying and recording, or in any information storage or retrieval system, is forbidden without the written permission of the editorial office, Silhouette Books, 300 East 42nd Street, New York, NY 10017 U.S.A.

All characters in this book have no existence outside the imagination of the author and have no relation whatsoever to anyone bearing the same name or names. They are not even distantly inspired by any individual known or unknown to the author, and all incidents are pure invention.

This edition published by arrangement with Harlequin Books S.A.

® and TM are trademarks of Harlequin Books S.A., used under license. Trademarks indicated with ® are registered in the United States Patent and Trademark Office, the Canadian Trade Marks Office and in other countries.

Visit Silhouette at www.eHarlequin.com

Printed in U.S.A.

CHARLOTTE HUGHES

is a romance and comedy author who has published over thirty critically acclaimed novels. She is a comic Southern writer and lives in antebellum Beaufort, South Carolina, with her two dachshunds, whom she lovingly refers to as "Dumb" and "Dumber."

Charlotte began her career with writing short romantic novels. More recently she has been writing romantic suspense books, for which she won two Maggie Awards, while a third book was a finalist. She also writes comic romance for MIRA Books, and *Hot Shot* will come out in September 2003.

To my brother, David Anthony Neal, with much love.
I still believe in miracles.

One

She was sleeping beneath her wedding dress, a mountain of satin and crinoline and a mile-long train. Neil Logan shook his head sadly at the sight.

"Okay, Katie. Come out from under there, or I'm coming in after you."

The dress seemed to take on a life of its own, going into a slow bump-and-grind routine as the woman wormed her way out. A mane of blond hair appeared, framing a flushed, sleepy-eyed face. She peered up at the man in tight, faded jeans and matching jacket and groaned. "Oh, Lord, it's Satan. Go away."

"One…"

"Beat it, Logan."

"…two…three." He grasped two slender wrists and tugged.

Katie muttered a four-letter word as she struggled to free herself from his grasp, but it was useless. He pulled her from beneath the dress, exposing her backside to the chilly air in her bedroom. "Dammit, Neil!"

Neil arched his dark brows as he took in Katie's attire— a wispy bra and gossamer panties that exposed the small of her back and a perfect rump. He swallowed. What had happened to the six-year-old his parents had taken in after her mother died? Gone was the skinny little girl with braces and knobby knees. He gave a low whistle. "Nice butt, Miss Jones."

She shrieked, quickly sat on the floor and pulled the gown to her breasts. Her pretty features wore a look of pure indignation. "Who do you think you are, barging into my bedroom like this, you…you…"

"Pervert? Hound from hell?" He crossed his arms over his broad chest and leaned against the wall, a glint of humor in his eyes. "What I'd like to know is, whatever happened to those shapeless flannel gowns and furry bunny-rabbit bedroom shoes you used to wear?"

He loomed over her—six feet, two inches of brawny male—wearing a grin that a girlfriend of hers claimed could melt a woman's bones. Katie suspected he used it to his advantage every chance he got. "How did you get into my house?" she demanded.

"Grabbed your key from beneath one of your flowerpots. How original, Katie. It's people like you who keep me in a job. Of course, I knocked and rang the doorbell first, but there was no answer."

"I suppose it never entered that thick skull of yours that I didn't wish to be bothered."

He lifted one corner of his mouth slightly. "Now you've gone and cut me to the quick, squirt, what with that razor-sharp tongue of yours."

"Don't start with me, Neil. I'm not in the mood. And don't call me squirt. I'm not a kid anymore. I'm twenty-nine years old, almost thirty." She knew she was being

3 1833 04308 8175

unkind, but what could people expect after what she'd been through? She had specifically told everybody she wanted to be alone, but the telephone hadn't stopped ringing in the twenty-four hours since she'd locked herself in her house and pulled the drapes closed. How like Neil to just barge into her bedroom as if he had every right. And try to get a free peek at what she *wasn't* wearing while he was at it.

Some things never changed. He was still a scoundrel. She pointed to the door. "Go!"

Neil stared at her, noting the mussed hair that brushed past her shoulders. The color reminded him of buttercups. And her glistening eyes—a brilliant emerald color that flashed when the light caught them just right. "Katie, Katie, Katie. Is that any way to talk to the man who was sent here to rescue you?"

"I don't need rescuing. I'm perfectly capable of taking care of myself."

"Have you looked into a mirror lately? Your hair is all over the place, your mascara is smudged and your eyes are red and puffy. Why, you look worse than some of the women I've dated."

"That's scary, Neil."

He made a "tsking" sound, but Katie saw a look of pure amusement in his eyes. "And you've wrinkled your wedding dress that, no doubt, cost half my inheritance. I hope it'll keep me warm when I'm forced to live in my car."

She was in no mood for his teasing, which is what Neil did best when she found herself in a predicament. As sole heir of a magazine dynasty, he had about as much chance of living out of his car as a member of the Kennedy family. Nevertheless, she wanted to cry at the sight of her gown. Neil's mother had designed it, a dress fit for a queen, although Katie had thought it a little much for a commoner like herself. It had been showcased in *Bride Magazine* and the society column in the *Atlanta Journal and Constitution*.

Now the dress was an amorphous lump. Katie pulled it to her chin.

Neil dropped down beside her on one knee, resting his hands on the other one. His heavy-lidded gaze met hers. "You don't have to hide behind the dress, sweetheart. Sexy underwear doesn't turn me on. My tastes are more…eclectic."

Katie could only imagine. "Gee, I'm sorry to hear that, Neil, but the lingerie store was out of whips and chains." He shot her another disarming grin. The man had no shame. He was a good seven years older than she, but one would never have guessed it. Mother Nature had been good to Neil Logan. He was lean and muscular, with a fine network of lines on either side of his eyes, barely noticeable beneath a deep-olive complexion. His hair was still dark, the color of Brazil nuts, without the first hint of gray, curling well past his collar. The thick stubble on his jaw was black as tar, giving him a dangerous look that appealed to women. And Neil had had his share of admirers. Katie had been thirteen years old when she'd developed a crush on him. But he hadn't noticed.

"Like what you see, Katie?"

She felt a blush creep up her neck. Neil assumed every female, including her, couldn't take their eyes off him. Smug was his middle name. True, he was about as handsome as they came, in a rugged, tough-guy sort of way, but she preferred a more polished look. "Actually, I was just about to ask if you'd lost your razor."

"I shaved for your wedding. Just keeps growing right back."

"Sounds like a testosterone thing."

"I'm just oozing with it, baby. Besides, I can't afford to look too clean-cut. I'm on a case."

"Which side of the law are you working for this time?"

"I'm one of the good guys."

He didn't look like it with his clothes as ratty as something plucked from a rag bin. A direct contrast to his father, who wore Armani suits, carried a Gucci briefcase, and purchased a new Mercedes every two years. Father and son had never seen eye-to-eye. Neil had been groomed to take over the family magazine, but he'd shown absolutely no interest. Instead he'd become a cop. Obviously a good one, he'd made detective at thirty.

"I really need to be alone, Neil." Katie sniffed.

"Oh, so you're going to turn this into a real pity party. Wish I had known. I could have brought cheap wine, dead flowers and black helium balloons. We could have done it up right."

A single tear slipped down her cheek. She had tossed fitfully through the night, and what little sleep she'd had, had not deadened the raw hurt and humiliation she'd felt when Drew hadn't shown up at the church. She still remembered the looks of embarrassment and pity on her bridesmaids' faces, the sorrowful expression in Neil's mother's eyes. It had reminded her of another time—when her mother had died, and she'd had no one, not one single relative to claim the illegitimate orphan. Poor little Katie Jones, they'd all said. Well, she hadn't wanted anyone to feel sorry for her then, and she didn't want it now.

"I'm not having a pity party, as you call it," she replied. "I'm just trying to decide what to do. I've sold my house and put most of my belongings in storage. I have no place to go." She had screwed up royally, only this time she had more than herself to consider.

Neil's look softened. Katie could raise his ire quicker than anyone he knew, but he realized this was not the time to get into a battle of wills. "Look, kiddo, it's not the end of the world. If I told you how many times I've been dumped—"

"Give me a break. You've never been dumped. You're

the one who always walks away from a relationship because you can't handle commitment."

"I was dumped in first grade by Marcie Henderson, but that was before your time."

"I love Drew."

"He's not good enough for you. I think he figured it out in the end, and that's why he pulled a no-show."

Another tear. "You're wrong, Neil. Drew's a good man with a bright future." Katie had no idea why she was taking up the cause for the skunk, but she was not about to let Neil think she'd almost married a loser. "Why, he's honest and decent and caring and...and..."

"And drinking those cute little umbrella drinks with another woman in Jamaica right now."

Katie couldn't hide her astonishment. "I don't believe you."

"You have that option."

She stared at him. He wasn't kidding. "How do you know that?"

"I have ways of finding out. Your fiancé used the airline tickets and honeymoon package my mom and dad gave you as a wedding gift, only he didn't board the plane alone."

Katie froze as a multitude of emotions ran through her: shock, denial and finally a scalding fury that seemed to vibrate through her body. She felt as if the breath had been knocked out of her. "Who is she?" Her voice was barely audible.

"I don't have the details. Besides, what does it matter at this point?"

Katie suspected Neil knew exactly who had climbed on that plane with Drew, but he would never tell her. He could be as closemouthed as they came. "Thanks for nothing," she muttered.

"You have to move on, kiddo. Maybe it's time you realized love is not all it's cracked up to be."

"What do *you* know about love?"

"Oh, I know all about love. I've seen what happens when it goes bad."

She imagined he'd seen enough domestic violence in his career to last a lifetime. "How about when love goes good, Neil? Have you looked at your parents lately? They've been married for forty years now, and they're just as much in love today as they were when they first married." She didn't give him a chance to respond. "You've hardened. You automatically think everybody in the world is bad. I prefer to think most people are kind and decent at heart. When you expect the best of people you usually get it."

He cocked his head to the side. "Is Drew one of the good guys, Katie? And how about your old man, who walked out on your mother the minute he found out she was pregnant?" Neil saw her flinch and wished he could take back his words. "Hey, I'm sorry I said that." But it was too late. The ice-cold look in her eyes told him he'd gone too far.

"Thank you for putting me in my place, Neil."

He let out a sigh of pure frustration. "I said I was sorry, but dammit, Katie, you have a tendency to bring out the worst in me. I don't know why I even bothered to come here."

"Why did you?"

"Because my parents sent me. They're worried sick about you."

"I've called them twice," she said defensively. "I plainly told them I just needed to be alone for a little while. I need time to get over this, and I don't want June and Richard fussing over me and making things worse. You know how they are." Her eyes misted. "Besides, I've embarrassed them. All those wedding showers and gifts and parties. And all those people in church, witnessing *firsthand* my mortification when the groom didn't show. I'll never be able to make it up to your parents after all they've done for me.''

''*You* haven't done anything wrong,'' he said. ''And the only thing my parents are feeling right now is a great deal of relief that you didn't marry the bastard.'' Neil saw the dress had slipped off one shoulder. He caught sight of Katie's bra and one enticingly erect nipple. He knew he should be ashamed of himself for noticing, but hell, how could he help it? Little Katie Jones had turned into a beautiful woman, almost overnight. ''How come it's so cold in here?'' he asked.

''The utilities were cut off yesterday. I wasn't planning on coming back. The new owners are taking possession tomorrow.'' Katie covered her face with her hands. ''My life is such a mess. Most of my clothes are at the new house. The one Drew and I were to share after our honeymoon,'' she added miserably. ''The others are in suitcases sitting in Drew's trunk. Unless his new girlfriend decided to take them *as well as* my fiancé.''

''My source didn't mention Drew was forced to board that plane at gunpoint.'' He was rewarded with a dark look. ''Things could be worse. You could have sold your bookstore like Drew wanted and invested the money in one of his get-rich-quick schemes.''

''How do you know about that?'' Katie asked. It wasn't as if they shared confidences. The only time she saw Neil was on holidays or other special occasions that involved family get-togethers. He had simply drifted in and out of her life for as long as she could remember, barely acknowledging her. Katie tolerated him; his mother made excuses. But neither one had been too happy when Neil had not shown up for Katie's engagement party.

''Like I said, I have ways.'' Neil would not mention that his mother had told him of Drew's request and asked him to check the guy out. The man had been clean, but that didn't mean he had Katie's best interests at heart. Her bookstore meant everything to her.

"I'll never sell my store," she said. "Not for Drew or anyone else." Which was true. Katie had bought the store out of foreclosure, using the money from her mother's insurance policy that the Logans' attorney had put into a trust fund for her. With the exception of Christmas and Thanksgiving, she'd worked seven days a week for the first two years so as not to miss a single customer.

It had paid off. Five years later she'd purchased the attached building. Not only had she gained more space for her beloved books, she'd installed a small kitchen and lunch area where people stood in line for her gourmet coffees and specialty sandwiches. Authors, even the big names, were more than happy to accept her invitations to book signings.

And then Drew Hastings had walked into her life. It was love at first sight, and after a six-month courtship, they'd become engaged. All her dreams had come true. She would finally have a family of her own.

Or so she'd thought.

Neil noted her sad look. "You okay?"

Katie was determined not to start crying again. "Neil, I realize I have a lot to be thankful for. I have people who care about me, and I have my store, but—" she swallowed "—I'm not ready to face anyone just yet."

Neil could see that she was in pain, and something inside tugged at his gut. "You need to go home, Katie," he said, his usual matter-of-fact tone becoming gentle. It was the tone he used when he pulled frightened, cowering children from crack houses and domestic violence, the same voice he used when little ones watched one or both parents being led away in handcuffs. And sometimes, no matter how hard he fought it, some of their pain seeped inside and became his.

Katie shook her head emphatically. ''Your mother won't give me a moment's rest, and you know it. She'll insist on dragging me to teas and plays and luncheons, and I'm simply not ready for that.''

''Can you stay with a friend?''

''That would be worse. They'll expect me to attend parties, and they'll try to set me up with their male friends, even though that's the last thing on my mind, thank you very much.''

''You can't stay here, Katie.''

''I'll go to a hotel.''

''Bad idea.''

''You got any better ones?''

Neil was growing weary. He'd been working a rape case for weeks that had turned personal when an elderly woman became the latest victim. He did not like becoming emotionally involved with a case, because it distorted his thinking. He wanted the facts and nothing more. Facts solved cases, and he was damn good at solving cases.

He and his partner had acted on a hunch last night and caught the guy at 2:00 a.m. Neil had spent three hours interrogating him before the man confessed. They'd booked him at dawn, and Neil had driven home looking forward to a little shut-eye. He'd managed to get in about three hours before his mother called about Katie.

''Come to my place,'' he said, suppressing a yawn. The words were out of his mouth before he realized it. Now, what had made him go and say something like that? Fatigue, probably. The last thing he needed in his life was a heartbroken female, one who got under his skin faster than a chigger bite. But he knew she would rip out her lungs with her own teeth before asking for help.

Her jaw dropped. "Your place? Are you out of your mind?"

He must be. But he was tired and hungry, and he wanted to be done with it, at least temporarily. Once he rested, he would be able to think more clearly. "What's wrong with my place? You've never even seen it."

Katie knew he had purchased a home in the last year, but she had no idea what it looked like or where it was located. "You've never invited me."

"I am now." When she hesitated, he went on. "Look, I'm in no mood to argue with you. Mom sent me here with strict orders to bring you home. She doesn't want you alone at a time like this. So you have a choice. I either take you there or I take you home with me for the time being."

"Why can't people just leave me alone?"

She looked so miserable that Neil cursed his own impatience. Katie was hurting, and she had every right. No matter what he personally thought of Drew Hastings, she loved the man, and people couldn't expect her to get over it in one day.

Finally he reached for her hand. It felt so tiny. He'd forgotten how delicately she was built, as she had such a presence. And her strength amazed him. He still remembered the day his parents had stood on either side of her and announced she was coming to live with them. He knew it hadn't been easy for her, what with just losing her mother and the only family she had. But she'd stood there, her tiny chin hitched high, shoulders squared, as though she were doing the family a big favor by agreeing to move in.

June and Richard Logan hadn't thought twice about taking her in. Not only had Katie's mother been a devoted employee for more than a decade, she had risked her life years before, pulling three-year-old Neil from the family pool, despite the fact she could not swim. That she had the sense of mind to immediately administer CPR had saved his life.

His parents had never forgotten. When Sara Jones gave birth to a baby out of wedlock, they'd not only helped out financially, they'd offered to be godparents.

Now Neil could only try to reason with Katie. "Like you said, people care about you. You're not in this alone."

Katie stared at the big warm hand holding hers. It was strong and brown and the back was feathered with dark hair. He had never shown her affection, and now she felt uncomfortable with it. At the same time, she experienced an odd sensation of feeling protected. And something else. Was it what people referred to as sexual magnetism? Was this the same flux of energy that drew women to him like hungry fish to a baited hook?

Confused, and more than a little flustered, she pulled her hand away and crossed her arms. Neil's eyes darkened as she withdrew.

Katie obviously didn't want him touching her. She had no idea how difficult it was for him to make such a gesture, and it irked Neil that she'd pulled away from his one attempt to offer comfort. "Make a decision, Katie," he said, his voice terse. "Where do you want to go?"

Katie tried to pull her thoughts together. None of her choices sounded particularly appealing. "You and I wouldn't last twenty-four hours under the same roof, and you know it."

Neil suspected she was right. "You're in a jam, and I'm offering to help. Simple as that."

"I'll be in the way. What if you should decide to entertain some young sweet thing?"

"I'll try to be discreet if you'll promise not to be so disagreeable."

"I resent that remark."

"See what I mean? Get dressed, and let's get out of here.

We can fight on the way back to my place. You're going to love Bruno.''

"Bruno? Are you living with a professional wrestler?"

"He's my dog. He loves women and cheese." He stood and reached for her hand. She hesitated. "Come on, let's go."

When she continued to just sit there, he became impatient. "Look, Katie, I have a life, and I'm not going to spend it watching you mope."

"I don't have any clothes."

He'd forgotten. "You don't have *anything?*"

She pointed to the gown. "This is it. No clothes, no money, nothing."

"How'd you pay the taxi driver after you raced out of church?"

"I didn't. He felt so sorry for me after I told him what happened that he didn't charge me for driving me here."

His frustration was growing. "Surely you have an old coat lying around?"

"I don't even have a bath towel."

He looked at the dress and then wiped his hand down his face. All he wanted was a few hours of sleep. "Katie, please put on the dress so we can get out of here."

"Oh, this is great!" she muttered. "Just great." Katie leaped to her feet, so angry she'd forgotten how little she wore. "My only hope is that all my neighbors will be home so they can witness the fact that Katie Jones has sunk to new levels of humiliation."

Neil couldn't speak for staring. One raking gaze convinced him she was the best thing he'd ever laid eyes on. He drank in the sight like a man who has thirsted for a long time. His body reacted immediately, a curious swooping pull in his gut that had no place to go but downward. The once-chilly room suddenly felt too warm for his skin.

He mentally chided himself for noticing. Hell, he and Katie had grown up together.

Katie was oblivious to the whole thing as she fussed with the dress. Lord, there was enough crinoline and satin to clothe a small town. What had June been thinking? She gritted her teeth as she tried to find the opening in the back. "In fact, I will be the yardstick by which all humiliation in Atlanta will be measured." Finally she found the back of the dress and tried to step inside. "Neil?"

"Huh?"

His voice sounded strained. Katie looked over her shoulder and blushed profusely when she caught him staring. She half turned, stood there for a moment, utterly speechless, as the room seemed to shrink in size, and the man before her became larger than life. It reminded her of when she was thirteen and thought herself madly in love with him. His steady gaze bore into her wide eyes. What was going on here? she thought, trying to quell the dizzy current racing through her veins. She realized she was holding her breath. She exhaled, and hot air gushed from her lungs.

Katie drew herself up sharply. This would not do; it simply would not do. Neil was more like a brother to her, and she was supposed to be in love with another man. No doubt she was still feeling the sting of rejection. That was the only excuse she had for feeling this…this surge of excitement over the fact that Neil Logan was staring. Her flesh prickled, and she was tempted to hide behind the dress again, but that would only draw attention to what was best left ignored. Besides, Neil Logan liked women, and the fact they'd grown up together obviously didn't matter at the moment. The only problem Neil had with women was committing to them.

"Do you think you could help me into my dress?" she asked, her voice giving nothing away.

"Oh, yeah." Somehow, Neil managed to get her inside

the contraption, although his fingers trembled as he zipped the back. He tried to think of something else, like the time she'd fallen off her bicycle, scraped both knees, and he'd had to carry her home while she wailed like a banshee. She'd been ten years old, he seventeen. She'd liked dolls and playing house. He'd been playing house since he was sixteen, only in a different way.

Back off, Logan, he told himself. *She's still a kid as far as you're concerned, and the closest thing you've ever had to a sister. You're way out of line thinking about her body.* "Where are your shoes?" he asked, noting his mouth had gone dry. He couldn't have rallied up a drop of spit if his life depended on it.

"I kicked them off when I chased the taxi. Besides, we'd never be able to find my feet in all this material. If you could just do something with this train, it would help."

He fumbled with it. Women were so much trouble. "I can't find the end of the damn thing."

"I don't think it ends. Your mother insisted it be as long as the Brooklyn Bridge. It hooks into the fabric, but there must be hundreds of them, and they're so tiny you'd need a magnifying glass. It'll take forever to unhook them." She could not imagine his large fingers managing such a feat.

"This is the most ridiculous thing I've ever seen," he grumbled, once again remembering how tired he was. Neil tried to wad the train into a big ball. Sweat beaded his brow. He was hard as stone and trying his best to pull his thoughts together, at the same time wondering why Katie insisted on talking so much. Yammer, yammer, yammer. Damned if women didn't go on and on once they got started. Hadn't he read somewhere that women talked three times more than men? He almost preferred it when Katie moped. At least she was quieter.

Once Neil locked up, they started for the car, with him muttering under his breath.

"What are you grumbling about back there?" Katie asked, trying to hold her skirt off the ground.

"I'm wondering why women insist on going to all this trouble with weddings when the divorce rate is so high."

She turned abruptly, and he bumped into her. "That sounds like something you would say. You want to know why we do it? I'll tell you why. Because some of us still believe in true love and happily-ever-after. Some of us want homes and babies, but that probably sounds foolish to a man like you."

"You want babies?" he asked in disbelief.

She blinked at him. "Of course I do. Surprised?" She flounced around and made for the car, and he followed, shaking his head.

Somehow Neil managed to get Katie inside his Jeep Wrangler, although her dress filled the entire front seat and bunched up to her nose. He tried to shove it aside as he climbed in on the other side. He had seen a lot of strange things in his life, but this beat them all. Still, she was a beautiful bride, despite her mussed hair and smudged eye makeup. He tried to imagine her image on top of a wedding cake and smiled.

She tossed him a dark look. "Okay, I know I look dumb as cow dung sitting here. Go ahead and get your chuckles so we can be on our way."

He tried to look serious, but he could feel one corner of his lip twitching. "I've never sat this close to a bride."

She glared at him. "Hellooo!" she shouted. "I'm not a bride. Remember? I was jilted? Left at the altar?"

Neil winced as he started the engine. "Would you stop screeching before you shatter both my eardrums *and* my windshield?"

"I wasn't screeching. May I roll down my window? I'm not feeling well."

He lowered it for her. "You need to calm down."

"Calm down?" she asked, as he backed from her driveway. "I haven't eaten in more than twenty-four hours, I slept on a cold floor last night, and I would kill for a cup of coffee. Oh, my Lord, there's Mrs. Henry walking her dog. She's the biggest gossip in the neighborhood." Katie ducked. "Did she see me?"

"Are you kidding? *I* can't even see you." They rode in silence for a while as he pondered his situation. Two or three days should do it until Katie came up with a plan. Surely that was all she needed to get her act together and find a place. Just to be nice, he'd give her a week.

One week. Seven days—168 hours.

It sounded like a life sentence.

Two

They hadn't gone very far when Katie began squirming in her seat. "Neil?"

"Yeah?"

"I have to use the bathroom so badly my toes hurt."

"Now?" He looked at her. "In that get-up?"

"Trust me. I wouldn't put myself through more embarrassment if I thought I could hold it."

Neil muttered a curse and wheeled into the parking lot of a convenience store. Women! It was always something. "Okay, go for it."

Katie glanced out the window. At least the parking lot was empty, except for one car in the back, which probably belonged to the clerk. She looked at Neil as she reached for the door handle. He simply sat there. "Aren't you going to help me?"

Neil cut the engine and tapped his fingers against the steering wheel, staring at the double glass doors leading inside the store, his jaw muscles tight. He could feel the beginnings of a headache, and he silently cursed his mother for sending him over to get her. "Sure, Katie." He climbed out, made to close the door, then froze, his trained eye taking in the scene inside the store in a split second—man in hooded cap, clerk stuffing money into a bag. He reached inside and pushed Katie down. She opened her mouth to protest, but Neil covered it with his hand. "Shut up and don't move!"

Wide green eyes stared up in alarm.

"The store is being robbed," he said, removing his hand. "Stay down. Use my cell phone and call 911." He hit the master lock on the door and closed it quietly. He approached the store, crouching behind an outside ice machine in order to keep from being seen. He checked the situation, looking for a weapon. The hooded man had his hand in the pocket of his jacket, which the woman eyed nervously as she pulled money from the cash register. Neil pulled a gun from the back of his jeans and started for the door.

Katie remained in her crouched position, raising her head just high enough so she could see over the dashboard.

Neil flung open the glass door leading inside the store. "Freeze!" he yelled.

The man ran through the door of the convenience store, escaping Neil's grasp by a fraction of an inch. Neil ran after him, warning him to stop, even as the man darted into an alley.

Katie suddenly remembered the cell phone. Her hands trembled as she dialed. She would never make it as a cop; she was worthless when it came to emergencies. Finally someone answered. Katie started to say something when she suddenly heard a succession of shots in the distance. "Oh, my God!" she cried.

It was difficult to hear the voice on the other end with

her heart pounding and blood roaring through her ears. "Help!" she cried. "A friend of mine just walked into a robbery in progress. He's a detective with the APD. I just heard gunfire. He may have been—" she gulped "—shot!"

"Ma'am, calm down," the man on the other end said, "and give me the detective's name and location."

Katie realized she was hysterical, but she did her best to give him the information he requested. "Please hurry," she begged, imagining Neil lying on the sidewalk, riddled with bullets. She tossed the phone aside and pushed herself up from the seat.

What to do, what to do? She fretted for a moment. It felt like an hour had passed since she'd called, but she knew it had only been a matter of seconds. She glanced around, looking for some sign of a police car. Nothing. Neil could be dying.

Katie reached for the door handle. Neil had locked her in. She fumbled with the automatic lock, wrenched the door open and literally fell from the car when her knees refused to support her. Luckily there was enough crinoline beneath her dress to protect her from a fall from Mount Everest. She tried to gather her train and skirt about her. No easy task. Finally she tossed the train aside, and it trailed behind her as she raced for the alley, trying to prepare herself for what she might find. It was empty. She moved on, trying to stay near the wall and duck behind garbage cans, just as she'd seen policemen do on TV. *Try to be inconspicuous,* she told herself, though she knew it was impossible in her present attire.

Katie hadn't gone very far when her heel came into contact with something sharp. The pain was excruciating, radiating up her calf. She cried out and came to a screeching halt. Probably she shouldn't look. If her pain was any indication, then she'd undoubtedly cut off half her foot. She wrestled with her skirts, knowing she couldn't put it off.

She paled at the sight. A large shard of glass had sliced into her heel and was deeply lodged.

I'm going to faint, she thought as blood oozed from the fresh wound. She took a deep breath and yanked the glass. Blood spurted. She suddenly felt dizzy. She wavered, lost her balance and fell against a garbage can, knocking several others over in the process. She landed on her fanny, and another can toppled, dumping refuse in her lap—coffee grounds, a can of tomato juice, an open tin of sardines and a container of chocolate chip ice cream that had long since melted. She gagged at the smells as she tried to brush the garbage from her skirt. She covered her mouth, trying to breathe as little as she could. "Why me?" she asked, choking back tears.

The sound of footsteps startled her. Neil hurried along the alley with a boy who looked to be no more than thirteen or fourteen years old, his hands cuffed behind him. Katie cried out her relief. "You're alive!" she said. "I thought you'd been shot."

Neil came to a dead stop when he saw her. A menacing frown clouded his otherwise handsome face. "What the hell are you doing out here?" he demanded, almost growling the words. "I specifically told you—"

So he was angry. Big damn deal. She had more important things to worry about. "I'm bleeding to death, Neil, that's what I'm doing. I just hope I die fast because I can't take any more."

His eyes roved over her, and an even deeper frown creased his forehead as he caught sight of her foot. Blood streamed into the dirt. "Oh, that's great, Katie," he said, voice filled with sarcasm, "just great."

"I'm sorry if I've inconvenienced you from playing cops and robbers, but don't give this a second thought. I can hail a cab to the hospital. Hopefully, they'll have my blood type on hand because I'll need a couple of gallons. No problem.''

His jaw was hard. "I'm on official police business, Katie. You had no right following me." He glanced at the kid. "Sit."

"Yes, sir." The boy instantly dropped to the ground. His eyes were wide; he was obviously scared.

Neil handed Katie the gun as he knelt before her. "If the kid moves, shoot him in the kneecaps."

"What!"

"And keep quiet. I don't have time for this nonsense."

Katie knew it was best to do as he said. She grasped the gun tightly, although her hands shook so badly it was all she could do to keep from dropping it. Her fear subsided when she saw Neil had put the safety on.

"Dammit, Katie, you've sliced the hell out of it," Neil said. He pulled a pocketknife from his jeans.

"You're not going to hurt her, are you, Officer?" the boy asked.

"Shut up," Neil ordered, cutting a strip of material from the train of Katie's dress.

"Your mother is going to kill me," she wailed, earning a dark look from Neil as he applied pressure to the wound.

Tears streamed down her cheeks as she tried to keep her nausea at bay. "Why do you have to be so mean? I chased after you because I thought you'd been shot."

He looked up. "Shot? Why would you think that?" He began winding the material tightly around her heel and ankle.

"I heard gunshots."

"You heard firecrackers. This kid's pals thought it would be funny to shoot them off to distract me." He looked at the boy. "Your buddies are lucky to be alive right now. If I had mistaken the sound of firecrackers for gunshots—" He paused and shook his head. "But I'll tell them personally when I pick them up for interfering with an officer in pursuit. And you're going to supply me with their names, big shot.'' The boy looked away as Neil tied a knot to hold the fabric in place. ''That should do it until we get help, but you're going to need stitches.'' He shook his head and gave a weary sigh. ''Did you at least make the call like I asked you to?''

Katie nodded but remained quiet. She didn't blame him for being angry with her. She had acted irrationally by going after him. Had the situation been different, she might have put him at risk, but the thought that he could have been seriously injured had outweighed all logical thought. ''I'm sorry, Neil.''

''Sorry doesn't get it, Katie. You could have put both of us in danger.'' Sirens whined in the distance. ''Well, help is on the way,'' he said, avoiding eye contact. Neil had never been able to stay mad at her for long. He took the gun.

All at once the mouth of the alley was filled with police cars and flashing blue lights. Doors opened everywhere as uniformed cops crouched behind them, their weapons drawn. ''Hands behind your head!'' one of them shouted.

Neil looked at Katie. When she glanced away, he knew she had gone and done something else to make his life difficult. ''It's Logan,'' he called out. ''Everything's okay.''

The policemen hesitated. Finally, one of them shouted an order, and the men lowered their guns. A middle-aged man in plain clothes with a receding hairline approached them. ''You okay, Logan?''

Neil nodded at Dave Sanders, another detective with the force. ''Yeah, fine.''

''Dispatch said we had a man down. I almost wet my britches when I heard it was you. What the hell is going on?''

Neil looked at Katie. "What did you tell them?"

She refused to meet his gaze. "I told you I heard gunfire, and I thought you'd been...shot."

Neil muttered a four-letter word. He looked up at the officer. "There's been a misunderstanding, Dave."

Dave's eyes widened as he took in Katie. "Are you okay, miss? Or is it missus?"

Katie tossed him a dark look.

"She needs medical attention," Neil said.

"Hell's bells, Logan, we've got an ambulance, five squad cars and the rescue unit. Only thing missing is a chopper." He was grinning as he turned and called for a paramedic. Two young men rushed toward them with a black bag.

"We'd better get her over to the E.R.," one of them said after he'd examined Katie's heel.

"Could we hurry?" Katie asked. "I really need to use the ladies' room."

Neil stood, grabbing the boy by the scruff of his neck. "Go ahead and take her over," he said, "and strap her down or she'll have the whole hospital in an uproar. I'll be over as soon as I finish up here."

Katie gave him a dirty look, and he mimicked her. "I'll deal with you later," he said.

If Katie had been humiliated before, it was nothing compared to being wheeled into the emergency room in her filthy wedding gown. A kind nurse helped her to the ladies' room. Nevertheless, she could feel all eyes on her as she was taken back and examined by a Dr. Nettles.

Neil arrived shortly after Katie's heel had been stitched. He looked none too happy as she finished giving the receptionist her insurance information. Finally she was wheeled to Neil's car.

"I know you're angry with me," she said, noting the scowl on his face. "I was afraid for you."

"Let's just drop it, okay?" Neil rubbed the back of his neck. It wasn't yet two o'clock, and he felt as though he hadn't slept in a week.

"I'll find an apartment first thing in the morning. All I need is a ride back to your parents' house to pick up my car."

"You've got ten stitches in your heel. You can't walk or drive."

"I'll manage."

Neil stopped at a red light. "Look, could we just get through this day and discuss your plans in the morning? I'm beat, okay?"

"Fine." She crossed her arms and faced the side window.

The light changed, and he drove on. "And I'd appreciate it if you'd stop pouting, because I'm too tired to deal with it."

"I'm not pouting."

"I've seen you pout. I know that look."

She could feel her irritation growing. "I'm an adult. I do *not* pout."

"You pout if someone puts green peas on your plate, you pout if there's no ice cream in the house and you pouted when you wanted to get your ears pierced and Mom said you were too young."

"I was eleven years old. All the girls had pierced ears."

"You also pouted when she refused to let you shave your legs or wear makeup."

"I was disappointed, but I did *not* pout."

"You're pouting now."

Katie wondered how he could possibly remember the events. "You're just trying to pick a fight with me, Neil, but I refuse to be a part of it. I said I was sorry. What more do you expect?"

He glanced at her. "A little peace and quiet, maybe?"

They made the rest of the drive in silence.

Katie didn't quite know what to make of Neil's home, a sprawling ranch-style structure of stained, rough-hewn wood, situated on a large lot and surrounded by tall pines and hardwoods. He parked his Jeep, climbed out and made his way around to her door.

She opened it and started to step out, but the train had become tangled around her legs. Without a word Neil, once again, wadded the material into a large ball and lifted her off the seat. He slammed the door with one hip and carried her up the front walk. "I can manage," she said.

"Remember our deal? Peace and quiet." They hadn't reached the door before he heard a squeal of delight from the yard next door. He muttered another curse word under his breath as an elderly woman rushed over, smiling in delight.

"Neil Logan, you dirty dog, why didn't you tell me you were getting married?"

"Huh?" Neil suddenly realized how he and Katie must look. "Oh, no, I—"

"You skunk, you!" She smiled at Katie. "I'm Naomi Klumpet," she said, her smile fading slightly as she took in Katie's dress. "Dear, what on earth happened to you?"

"I was in…sort of an accident," Katie managed.

"Say what? You'll have to speak loudly, dear. I'm hard of hearing."

"An accident," Katie said, raising her voice.

"Oh, my word! And on your wedding day." She noted the bandage on Katie's foot. "I won't keep you. I can tell you're not feeling well." She sighed. "And with your wedding night ahead of you." She patted Katie's arm. "Please call me if you need something. Neil has my number.'' Naomi pinched his cheek hard.

''I wish you wouldn't do that, Mrs. Klumpet,'' he said, wincing.

''And you, young man, will have to answer to me later for keeping your marriage a secret,'' she replied.

''Mrs. Klumpet, wait—'' But the woman was halfway across his yard, and she would never hear him. Neil sighed, unlocked the door and carried Katie inside. She gave a shriek as an enormous black Labrador retriever bounded toward them. He pounced on Katie, digging his claws into her dress. She buried her face in Neil's jacket.

''Is he going to kill me?''

''Down, Bruno!'' Neil ordered. The dog dropped to the floor, looking remorseful. ''No, he doesn't bite. He's a big baby.'' Neil closed the door, carried her to the sofa and dropped her there unceremoniously. The dog sniffed her from head to toe as she remained motionless.

''Come on, Bruno, let's go out.'' Neil opened the back door, and the dog loped through it. Closing the door, Neil turned to Katie. He didn't look happy. ''This is great,'' he said. ''Just great. Naomi Klumpet thinks we're married. By nightfall she will have told the entire neighborhood. Tell me this, Katie. Do you ever have a normal day?''

''Never,'' she said. ''I get up every morning and try to think up new ways to screw up my life and everyone else who comes into contact with me.''

Neil didn't respond. Instead he disappeared into a hallway. A few minutes later he returned with a bathrobe. ''You need a bath. You stink.''

''Do you have a plastic bag and a rubber band? I should try to keep my bandage dry.''

He disappeared into the kitchen, returning a few minutes later with what she'd asked for. She stood and thanked him. ''The bathroom is down the hall. Let me help—''

"I'll be fine."

"Do me a favor. Don't lock the door. I can't take another mishap."

She ignored him and hobbled into the bathroom, as eager for a shower as Neil was for her to have one. She slipped off the gown and secured the plastic bag on her foot. A minute later she stepped under a hot spray of water, taking care not to put all her weight on her sore heel. She soaped herself all over and washed her hair twice. Her skin glowed when she stepped from the tub.

As she caught sight of her face in the mirror over the sink, she wished she had her purse and makeup. Her eyes were still puffy from all the crying she'd done the night before. June Logan probably had her personal belongings. Her purse and makeup had been the last thing on her mind when she'd bolted from the church. Once again a feeling of humiliation washed over her. She had handled it all wrong. She should have calmly asked June to help her out of her dress, allowed Richard to inform their guests the wedding was off and gone to the reception with her head held high as June had suggested. After all, the Logans had already rented the entire country club and flown in three-hundred live lobsters. No cost had been spared.

Katie felt like weeping, but surely she had no more tears left.

She finished toweling herself and slipped into Neil's bathrobe, which reached her ankles and would easily have fitted two of her. Somehow she had to get to the new house for her things. That brought a sigh to her lips. Thank goodness she and Drew had only leased the house. He'd wanted to hold off buying until they could afford to build in one of Atlanta's most exclusive neighborhoods. Katie would have settled for a less costly house, but Drew insisted they needed something especially nice. A stockbroker, he often entertained clients, and he wanted to be able to invite them to his home. To impress them.

Katie opened the bathroom door and hobbled down the hall to where Neil was preparing an early dinner. He frowned when he saw her. "Why didn't you call me?"

"I told you I could manage. Something smells good in here."

He didn't respond. Instead he turned to the coffeepot and poured her a cup. "I figured you could use this. Have a seat on that stool."

"Oh, bless you," she said, sitting down, at the same time trying to keep the bathrobe from falling open.

Neil placed a small pewter creamer and sugar bowl on a pewter tray in front of her. Several packs of artificial sweeter were tucked between the bowls. Katie arched both brows, impressed.

"A housewarming gift," he said.

Katie prepared her coffee the way she liked it and took a sip. "This is wonderful. She glanced over the counter and saw that he was preparing omelets. "When did you learn to cook?"

He looked at her and took a sip of his own coffee. His face was relaxed. "You'd be surprised what you can do when the alternative is going hungry. And I got tired of eating in restaurants." He gave her a slip of a smile. "Actually, an old girlfriend taught me. She thought it was time I got in touch with my feminine side."

Katie arched one brow. "Your feminine side?"

"Hey, I'm a sensitive guy. A new-millennium man."

"So, was it serious?" She wondered why she was interested.

"Of course not. This is me you're talking to."

"Oh, yes. The man who never met a woman with whom he wished to bond."

"You still like cinnamon-raisin toast?"

He remembered. They had eaten it as kids, but now she ate whole wheat. It seemed more sensible. "Love it."

He popped two slices in the toaster. "I hope you're not one of those women who insists on diet margarine, because I use only real butter."

Actually, everything she ate was low fat or sugar free, but she didn't think now was the time to mention it. Besides, she was too hungry. "I don't complain when someone else is doing the cooking. I feel guilty just sitting here."

"You can make it up to me when your foot heals. I'll start my list tonight."

She chuckled. "Do you have to go back to work?"

He shook his head. "I took the rest of the day off. It'll take that long for the department to stop laughing." He shot her one of his looks. The same look he'd given her the night she'd caught him sneaking in well after his curfew. He had been eighteen and hell-on-wheels at the time. She had just turned eleven and was intimidated by him so she'd kept quiet. Now, she simply shot him a look of her own.

"Just remember, I used to cover for you," she said.

"Yeah, you did, didn't you? I could never figure out the reason, since I wasn't exactly one of your favorite people."

"I got tired of hearing you and your father argue." She saw his eyes cloud over and decided it wasn't a good subject to pursue. "By the way, do you happen to have one of those big black lawn-and-garden bags?"

"Yeah, why? You intend to mow my grass while you're here?"

"I need to throw out my dress."

He eyed her. "Are you sure?"

"I've never been more sure of anything in my life. Besides, I don't want your mother to see it."

The toast popped up. Katie winced as Neil slathered a

hefty amount of butter on top, but she kept quiet. He lifted her omelet with a spatula, put it on the plate and handed it to her. "This looks delicious. What's in it?"

He shrugged. "Ham, cheese and onions. Nothing fancy. Go ahead and eat. Mine won't take but a minute."

As hungry as she was, she needed no further prompting. She tasted it. "You'll make some woman a fine husband." He simply grunted. "I remember a time when your idea of a meal was a can of Vienna sausage and a handful of crackers. Used to make Cleo so mad, especially when you ate over the sink."

Neil chuckled as he pictured his family's cook, now retired. "I still eat over the sink, only Cleo isn't here to smack the back of my head for doing it. By the way, I called my mom while you were showering. Told her you'd be staying here for a couple of days."

"What'd she say?"

"She advised me to empty my gun of bullets and hide all the sharp objects in the house."

"Sounds like they don't have much faith in us."

"Actually, she thought it was a good idea. Reporters have been calling the house all day."

Katie groaned. "I'll never live this down."

"That's not all. A reporter snapped a picture of you hightailing it from the church in your wedding gown and climbing into that cab."

The color drained from her face. "What do you suppose he'll do with it?"

"Nothing. Dad gave him five hundred dollars for the roll of film."

Yet another reason to feel guilty. "Why would someone take pleasure in another person's pain?"

"People enjoy reading about how the rich live. Especially if there's a scandal."

"I'm not rich."

"You were raised rich, and you stand to inherit a chunk of money one day."

Katie couldn't hide her surprise. "From your parents? Neil, I don't expect anything from them. I already have everything I need."

"Surely, it has occurred to you."

She shook her head. "Actually, no. Besides, I'm not a real member of the family."

Neil wondered if she was on the level. He realized he didn't know Katie as well as he thought. "They think of you as their daughter."

"Wouldn't you resent them for leaving me a portion of what belongs to you?" she asked, uncomfortable talking about it, at the same time thinking she should assure him she had no intention of taking what was rightfully his.

"Money doesn't interest me. If that's what I was about, I'd be sitting behind a desk in my dad's company right now."

"What *does* interest you?"

"Making a difference in this crazy world."

"Which is why you decided to become a cop."

"Much to my family's displeasure. But it's something I had to do, you know?"

She knew.

"You have a nice house," she pointed out, appreciating its simplicity. She wondered if he'd designed it that way because his parents' house had resembled a museum. There were too many things one could not touch, prized artifacts locked in glass cases, expensive Persian rugs with plastic runners that were not removed until company was expected. Neil's place was designed with comfort in mind.

"I saved for it and did some of the finishing work myself."

"You could have gone to your parents for the money."

"It wouldn't have meant as much."

Katie knew exactly where he was coming from. Her little house had been plain by most standards, but she'd adored it because she'd worked hard to save for the down payment. It was funny how the two of them had been raised in the lap of luxury but preferred simple things. They each had a generous trust fund; both of them could have afforded to drive luxury cars. Yet, Neil drove a Jeep Wrangler, and she'd bought her Toyota used.

Neil put his omelet on a plate and buttered two slices of toast. A bark sent him to the back door. Bruno hurried in and headed straight for Katie, sniffing her feet.

She curled her toes. "Are you sure he won't bite?"

"I told you, he loves women. He'll probably want to French kiss you before it's over." He glanced around. "So, you like my place?"

"Very nice. It could use a woman's touch, of course."

"I don't like clutter."

"I decorated my place very nicely, and it wasn't cluttered."

"I wouldn't know. You never invited me. But then, we don't exactly run in the same circles, do we?" He had no interest in joining the Arts Council or the Historic Society or Friends of the Library.

Katie didn't know whether to take offense at the remark. "We've always had separate interests. Besides, you were older and had your own set of friends."

"I was seldom home, Katie, if you'll remember correctly."

She knew he was referring to the years he'd spent in military school. She studied him, but his expression was closed. Neil Logan wasn't one to share his thoughts or feelings.

They ate in silence. Finally Neil got up and began clearing away the dishes. He finished loading the dishwasher and wiped the counters. "You'd probably like to see where you're sleeping."

"That would be nice. I might lie down for a little while. I didn't get much sleep last night."

Neil knew the feeling.

He helped her to her room, the look in his eyes giving nothing away. His touch was that of a stranger, helpful but impersonal.

Katie turned. "Thanks, Neil," she said. "For everything."

He nodded and closed the door.

Once he was gone, she climbed into the bed. She looked through his books, started reading a mystery but lost interest. She tried to sleep, but even as tired as she was, she couldn't turn off her thoughts. Worry plagued her. For someone who'd prided herself on keeping her life in order, she had failed miserably.

And the worst was still to come.

Katie opened her eyes the next morning and was surprised to find she'd slept a good twelve hours. She hadn't realized just how tired she had been, but she felt calmer and rested as she made her way cautiously toward the kitchen, taking care not to put pressure on her sore heel. She found Neil sitting at the kitchen counter drinking coffee, dressed in jeans and a leather jacket. He had not shaved, but it somehow enhanced his good looks. Not that she had any business noticing.

"Good morning," she said politely, hoping they could start the day off civilly.

Neil tried to avoid looking at her as she brushed by, but his eyes followed her every move. Damned if she wasn't a pretty sight in his oversize bathrobe, her skin flushed from sleep. He noted her slight limp. "How's the foot?"

"Sore, but it's better." She poured coffee into a mug, added cream and sweetener and sipped.

"I checked on you last night, but you were sleeping so soundly I decided not to wake you. I take it you were comfortable enough."

"Very." She realized they were conversing like two people who'd just met. She continued to sip her coffee in silence. It wasn't until she'd drunk half the cup that she was suddenly overcome by nausea. What in the world?

"Would you excuse me?" she managed, hobbling down the hall toward the bathroom. She closed the door and locked it, not a moment too soon. She lost her coffee, then spent the next few minutes suffering a bad case of dry heaves.

From the kitchen Neil heard her. He knocked on the bathroom door a few minutes later. Katie opened it, holding a washcloth to her face. She looked pale.

"Bad case of nerves, Katie?"

She met his gaze. Was it concern she read in his eyes? Katie owed him the truth. "Bad case of morning sickness, Neil. I'm pregnant."

Three

Neil stood there, stunned. "How far along are you?"

She hesitated. "Almost three months."

His look was incredulous. "Three months! And you haven't said anything?"

"I've only known for a few weeks. I was so busy planning this wedding, attending bridal showers and working at the store that I didn't even notice when I missed my first—well, you know…"

"Period," he stated flatly. "It's not a dirty word."

Maybe not, but she wasn't accustomed to discussing her female problems with Neil. "Then, when I missed my second…uh, period, which I really thought was my first, I checked my calendar. I bought a home pregnancy test. By the time I went to the doctor, I was two and a half months along."

"Weren't you experiencing morning sickness?"

"Rarely. I thought it was stress related, and everybody

I knew was passing around a stomach virus at the time. I figured I was having a tough time kicking it because I was so tired." She decided not to mention that her breasts hadn't become tender until recently. "My doctor says every woman is different."

"Drew knew you were pregnant, and he abandoned you at the altar anyway?"

More hesitation. "He didn't know. I'd planned to tell him on our honeymoon. He wanted to start a family right away. I wanted to surprise him."

Neil had heard Drew was anxious for kids, but he'd suspected the man had ulterior motives. Neil wiped a hand down his face. "This is great, Katie, just great. Why the hell didn't you tell me this yesterday?"

She hitched her chin high. "Because it doesn't concern you. It's my problem."

"So what are you going to do about it?"

"I plan to keep the baby and raise it myself." She hobbled to her bedroom and sat on the bed.

Neil followed her, stopping just outside her door. She was right; it didn't concern him. But he'd seen too many women struggle to raise their children on their own. Many of them lived in poverty because the fathers could not be found to help support the family. He knew Katie would never have to worry about money, but the thought of her going through the pregnancy alone, not to mention raising a child without benefit of a husband and father, wasn't a pleasant one.

"I think having the baby would be a mistake," he said finally. "A child needs a father." She didn't respond. "Katie, I've been out in the real world. Most crimes today are committed by young men who were raised without a father figure."

Katie met his gaze. His blue eyes were troubled, his lips pressed into a grim line. She sensed he wasn't as much upset with her as he was *for* her. "Your parents have been wonderful to me, Neil, and this is not intended to be disrespectful of them. It's just—" She paused and struggled with her emotions. "I've always wanted a family of my very own. It was so important to me that I missed all the warning signs when Drew walked into my life."

Neil began to pace. He'd never seen this side of Katie. He'd assumed she was perfectly happy with her career and friends and the many activities and causes in which she was involved. He should have guessed that she'd wanted more out of life when she'd allowed herself to become involved with Drew Hastings, but he hadn't said anything because…well, because he hadn't wanted to interfere in her life. Sure, he'd done his share of grumbling, he'd gotten downright pissed off. Drew wasn't good enough, in his opinion. Then, he'd wondered if anyone would have been good enough for her, as far as he was concerned. So he'd sat home and gotten drunk the night of her engagement party, instead of showing up and offering his congratulations.

"If that's your choice, fine," he said after a moment, "but before you make your final decision, I want you to think about what you'll be doing." He held up his hands before walking out.

Katie heard the front door close a moment later, but she continued to sit on the bed quietly. Bruno came to her door, his look mournful, as though he sensed a problem. He walked over to her and plopped his head on her knee. "At least you're on my side." Katie stroked his silky ears and hoped she was making the right decision.

The day dragged for Katie, who was accustomed to getting up early and opening her store by nine o'clock. The phone rang, and she checked the number on the caller ID before answering. The Logans' phone number flashed on the small screen. Katie knew she had to talk to them sooner or later. She picked up the phone. June Logan spoke from the other end.

"How are you today, dear?"

Katie tried to sound upbeat. "Much better, thank you. I appreciate you and Richard calling to check on me. I'm sorry I...fell apart like I did. I'll never be able to make this up to you and Richard. I know you spent a fortune on my wedding—"

"Don't give it a second thought, because we haven't," the woman admonished. "We're more concerned about your well-being."

Katie gave a mental sigh of relief. "I'm fine now, really. I just needed time to think. Neil has been wonderful about the whole thing."

"I'm thankful to hear it." June paused. "Katie, Drew wasn't good enough for you, and he knew it."

It was the second time she'd been told as much. "I really screwed up. I just wish he'd had the courage to back out sooner and save us all a lot of embarrassment."

"What's done is done. We miss you, dear, but you're probably better off at Neil's at the moment. This place is a madhouse, reporters calling, friends checking to see if you're okay and wedding gifts still arriving." Another pause. "I hate to bring this up, but I thought we should start returning them as soon as possible. There are literally hundreds still sitting on folding tables in the ballroom. Richard's secretary and another girl from the office have offered to come in and sort through them. Since there are so many, I thought we'd have a nice card printed up, thanking the giver, etc., etc., and put the cards with the gifts when we return them. It's all taken care of, so you needn't give it a second thought."

Katie felt as though a boulder had been rolled from her shoulders. One less thing to worry about, thanks to June, who would rather trample through a briar patch barefoot than have her friends think she was not practicing perfect etiquette when it came to social duties. But that's just the way she was, and she had drilled good manners into Katie at an early age. There was no excuse for missing a birthday or anniversary, and forgetting to send thank-you cards when someone did something kind was unconscionable.

"You always think of just the right thing," Katie said. "Thank you."

"You're welcome, dear. Oh, by the way, you need to telephone Genna. She's called several times. I told her you were with Neil and not to worry."

Genna Reynolds was Katie's best friend and employee. "I'll give her a call later."

"I love you, Katie."

Once again Katie struggled with her emotions. "I love you, too, June." She hung up a moment later, wondering how June would feel when she discovered the wedding gown was stuffed into a black garbage bag awaiting a trip to the dump and that Katie was pregnant, to boot.

When Neil arrived home at the end of the day, he was carrying Katie's suitcases and purse. Her mouth dropped open as Bruno raced to greet him.

"How did you manage to get my things?" she asked from the kitchen as she put the finishing touches on two salads.

He shrugged. "I checked Drew's license tag from the Department of Motor Vehicles, called airport security and had them look for his car in the long-term parking lot. Then, I stopped by Mom and Dad's and grabbed your purse and car."

"But how did you get into the trunk of Drew's car?"

"You ask too many questions. Just be glad I got them." He looked at the dog. "Do you need to go out?"

Katie was so thrilled to have her things she felt like hugging Neil. "I let him out a few minutes ago. He should be okay for now."

Neil nodded but didn't quite meet her gaze as he set her car keys on the kitchen counter. "I'll ride in with my partner in the morning and retrieve my car."

"You're incredible!"

He arched both brows. "Women don't usually tell me that until they get to know me a little better." He had the satisfaction of seeing her blush.

"It's just…you get things done. I've been wondering all day what I was going to do about my car and my clothes." She had not wanted to bother him with it, especially after their altercation that morning. "Not that I don't adore this bathrobe you lent me."

As cute as she looked in it, Neil would be happy to see her in something a little more formfitting. He pushed the thought from his head, knowing he had no business thinking about it. "What smells so good?"

"Meat loaf. You don't keep a lot of food on hand, so I worked with what I could find."

"You're supposed to stay off that foot."

"I know, but I can only stand so much inactivity. I need to go back to work."

He glanced around, noting the wood floors had been mopped. The table was set with cloth place mats and napkins, another housewarming gift he'd never taken out of the package. Her heel was going to hurt like hell tomorrow.

"Just like a woman to try and change things the minute she walks through a man's door. What can I do to help?"

"Stay out of my way."

"You got it." Neil walked into the living room and paused at the sight of a floral arrangement on a coffee table that had been waxed until it looked as though it had just come out of the carton. "Who sent the flowers?"

"Naomi Klumpet," she said, "with a card of congratulations on our new marriage. She's planning on giving us a party.'' She rolled her eyes heavenward.

Neil shook his head sadly, wondering what was next. He grabbed the remote control and turned on the TV set. He sat down on the sofa and flipped through several channels. But his mind wasn't on the programs. He'd thought about Katie all day, trying to figure out an answer to her problem. He'd almost called her a couple of times to see if she was okay, but had decided against it. Just as he'd decided to distance himself for the remaining time she was there.

''Dinner's ready,'' she announced some minutes later.

Neil jumped at the sound of her voice, chiding himself for being so edgy. If Katie noticed, she didn't say anything. ''Just give me a minute to wash up,'' he said.

Neil soaped his hands, staring at himself over the bathroom mirror as he did so. He was scowling, and he knew why. Not only was Katie driving him crazy, flouncing around in his bathrobe, which parted every so often, giving him a peek of the prettiest legs he'd ever seen. She had taken over his house, cleaning and cooking as though she'd been doing it for years. Why did women feel they had to make nests? It never failed. If a woman spent the weekend with him she thought it was up to her to redecorate the place and straighten his cabinets.

When he returned, he found Katie sitting quietly at the table, obviously waiting for him. The meat loaf she'd prepared looked appetizing, as did the bowl of mashed potatoes and another of green beans. He saw that she'd prepared two salads as well. ''I wish you hadn't gone to so much trouble,'' he said, taking his seat at the opposite end of the table. ''I'd planned to order a pizza.''

She looked up. ''I'm sorry. I didn't mean to take over your kitchen. I thought you'd enjoy a home-cooked meal. And—'' she shrugged ''—it was the least I could do.''

He'd managed to say the wrong thing, and now she was

apologizing for all the work she'd done. "I wasn't criticizing you, Katie, it's just…I don't expect all this."

They ate in silence. Neil tried to think of something to say. "Everything tastes great," he said at last.

"I'm glad you like it."

"You feeling okay? Other than the foot, I mean?"

She nodded. "Fine. And you?" She smiled, wondering why they were having so much trouble carrying on a simple conversation. One would have thought they were strangers sharing a meal for the first time.

They simply gazed at each other.

Katie noticed how good he looked in a navy T-shirt, stretched tight across his broad chest.

Neil thought she looked like a college girl, clean-scrubbed, her hair pulled into a ponytail. He wondered if she was wearing anything beneath his bathrobe, and he knew he had no business thinking along those lines.

"I'm okay." He decided to concentrate on his meal.

"I spoke with your mother today," Katie said after a moment.

"Oh?" He glanced up. Her look was pensive, her usually smooth forehead creased between her light brows. "Did you tell her?"

"No. She's got her hands full at the moment."

Neil put down his fork and shoved his plate aside. He'd suddenly lost his appetite.

Katie saw that he'd touched very little on his plate. "You didn't eat much."

"It has nothing to do with your cooking. I've got a lot on my mind right now."

"I wish I hadn't told you about the baby."

"This has nothing to do with you. It's work related." Neil was lying. He seldom thought about work when he came home, unless it was a particularly grisly case. He knew other cops who dwelt on their jobs and drank to forget but he refused to fall into that routine. So he worked out. It not only kept him in shape, it cleared his mind.

Katie ate her dinner in silence. "I was thinking of asking your parents to lunch tomorrow," she finally said. "I plan to break the news then. I'll call your mom tonight and see if they're free."

"Do you want me there?"

"That's not necessary. I'm sure you have enough to do at work."

Neil propped his elbows on the table. "That's not what I asked."

Katie fidgeted with her hands. "It would be nice having you there for moral support."

He knew it had been hard for her to admit she preferred having him with her when she broke the news. This was the same Katie who'd spent the night sleeping on the floor in a cold house rather than going to his parents' house and burdening them, the same girl who'd hung on to the worn coat her mother had bought her, rather than allow his parents to replace it with a nicer one. He'd never known a more stubborn and determined woman.

"All you had to do was ask," he said. "See how simple that was?"

Katie noticed the stares the minute she and Neil walked through the doors of one of Atlanta's most exclusive country clubs. The Logans had chosen to meet there in hopes of avoiding reporters. Neil kept glancing appreciatively in Katie's direction. She looked like a million bucks in a kelly-green silk suit and matching heels that he assumed she'd purchased for her honeymoon. It was impossible to believe she was almost three months pregnant. She'd insisted on wearing the shoes despite her sore heel, and he hadn't argued for fear she would think he was telling her what to do.

"Nervous?" he asked.

She gave him a tight smile. "Very. I'm just glad you're here." She was also glad he'd traded in his worn jeans for tan slacks and a navy blazer. Even his dress shirt was starched and ironed. She wasn't surprised when the hostess looked long and hard at him once they entered the restaurant area. He seemed not to notice.

June and Richard Logan greeted them warmly once the hostess delivered Neil and Katie to their table. Richard stood, as he always did when a lady approached, his manners as impeccable as his taste in fine wine and cigars. He looked refined in a dark silk suit. His salt-and-pepper hair was more salt than pepper, cropped neatly as always, never a hair out of place. They had chosen a table at the very back of the restaurant, as if they'd hoped for privacy. Katie kissed both of them on the cheek. Neil dropped a perfunctory peck on his mother's cheek before shaking his father's hand.

"Katie, you look absolutely stunning," June said.

"So do you," Katie replied. As always, June Logan looked as though she'd just walked from between the pages of a designer magazine, this time dressed in a smart, navy linen suit and a simple pearl necklace. She wore sophistication like a second skin.

"Is something wrong with your foot?" Richard asked once they sat down. "You looked as though you were limping when you came in."

"I cut my heel on a piece of glass. Nothing serious, but it's still a little sore." Actually, it hurt like the dickens in her new pumps, but dressing well had boosted her self-confidence, which she so desperately needed at the moment.

"I'm starved," Neil announced, changing the subject so his parents wouldn't ask for an explanation.

The waitress came to the table, handed them menus and

took a drink order. All four ordered iced tea, and their server hurried away to fill the order.

"It's about time you rejoined the living, Katie," Richard scolded gently. "We've been worried."

Katie shifted uncomfortably in her seat. "I'm sorry for making the two of you anxious. I needed a couple of days to lick my wounds."

June patted her hand. "We'll get through this. One day we'll all laugh about it."

"And Drew Hastings will never work in this town again," Richard said, surprising even Neil. He looked at Katie. "You can count on that. He has embarrassed this family for the first and last time."

Katie nodded, not knowing what to say. Richard Logan came from old money and was one of the most powerful businessmen in Atlanta. Katie had no doubt he would make mincemeat out of Drew's career before it was over.

"Dear, I know you mean well," June said to her husband, "but I don't think we should discuss this right now."

"You're right, June, but you know how I feel about what that SOB did to our Katie."

Katie smiled. Richard had been referring to her as *our* Katie for as long as she could remember. Their drinks arrived, and the waitress took their orders. Everyone agreed on a chef salad except for Neil, who ordered a prime rib sandwich and fries.

"I was surprised you chose to stay with Neil," Richard said to Katie.

"I thought it best under the circumstances." She flashed Neil a smile. "Your son has been very generous. His house is nice and comfortable."

"Oh?" Richard said. "You know, June and I have never seen it."

Katie saw Neil's jaw tighten and hoped the two men

would be civil to each other. "You're welcome anytime," Neil said.

"Your mother never goes anywhere unless she's personally invited."

"I'm surprised you and Neil haven't come to blows," June said with a light chuckle, as if she thought a change of subject were in order. "Heaven knows you didn't get along this well when you were younger."

Neil grinned. "Bruno keeps her in line."

"Your dog?" June asked.

"A black Lab," Katie said, laughing in spite of her nervousness. "He weighs more than I do. I was terrified of him at first. Until I discovered he's a big baby. Neil has spoiled him." She entertained them with some of the dog's antics.

"I see you have your clothes," June said.

Katie nodded. "Neil managed to get them out of the trunk of Drew's car. I plan to go out to the house later for the rest of my belongings." The older adults nodded. They knew which house Katie spoke of.

"Is your name on the lease?" Richard asked. When Katie nodded, he pulled out a thin notebook and scribbled in it.

"What are you doing?" June asked him.

"Just taking notes. I want all my information in front of me when I take Hastings to court and sue the socks off of him."

"How are you going to get money out of him if he has no job?" Neil asked.

Richard looked at him. "That will be up to my attorney. Do you think I should sit back and do nothing?"

"Taking him to court is too good for him," Neil replied. He grinned suddenly. "I know guys who would take him out for less than fifty bucks."

"I'll do it for free," Katie said.

June looked shocked. "My word! I can't believe what I'm hearing."

Richard shot his wife a remorseful look. "I'm sorry, honey. We won't speak of it again."

They made small talk until their food arrived. Katie told them what was going on at the store. "I spoke with Genna this morning. I feel guilty not being there, but it feels good to take a little vacation."

Lunch arrived, and June discussed plans for a fall bazaar to raise money for the battered-women's shelter.

"Does anyone want coffee?" Richard asked as they neared the end of their lunch.

Katie had seen him glance at his wristwatch a couple of times, and she sensed he was in a hurry. "I would like a cup of decaffeinated," she said quickly, hoping to stall for time. The others ordered theirs straight.

He motioned for the waitress, who hurried to the table. He placed the coffee order and asked for the check.

"Richard, I'm still eating my salad," June said.

"I have an appointment at one-thirty, hon, but the rest of you take your time, please."

Neil looked at Katie and nodded, prodding her on.

She cleared her throat. "June? Richard?" They both looked at her. The words froze on her lips.

June smiled pleasantly. "Yes, dear?"

"You don't know how much this lunch has meant to me."

Neil frowned. The Logans looked at one another. "We should do it more often," Richard said.

"Katie, don't you have something to tell them?" Neil asked.

The color drained from her face as she regarded the other couple. "Well, yes…"

"What is it?" Richard asked.

Katie clasped her hands together in her lap. "This isn't easy."

June cocked her head to the side, waiting. "Honey, you can tell us anything."

"Just say it, Katie," Neil mumbled.

"I know this wedding business has been a big disappointment to you both, and I can't tell you how sorry I am. I never meant for any of this to happen, and—"

"Katie, what *is* it?" Richard demanded.

"I'm pregnant."

June's jaw dropped.

"What?" Richard asked.

They looked up to find the waitress standing there. She smiled meekly. "Did I come at a bad time?"

"Just put the coffee on the table," Richard said, reaching into his jacket for a tiny cell phone. He punched a few buttons. "Jackie, cancel my one-thirty appointment." He punched another button and slipped the phone back into his pocket.

June leaned close. "Katie, are you sure about this?"

"Yes. I'm almost three months."

The woman gasped.

"Hastings is going to pay for this," Richard muttered under his breath. "Katie's a good girl. That scoundrel took advantage of her." He eyed Katie suspiciously. "Did he get you drunk or force you in any way?"

"No. I knew exactly what I was doing."

June and Richard looked shocked.

"Katie's almost thirty years old, for Pete's sake," Neil said.

They were silent as the waitress reappeared with the check and removed their dishes. Richard pulled out a credit card and handed it to her.

June pulled a linen handkerchief from her purse and

dabbed her eyes. "Oh, this is awful, just awful. Poor Katie. No husband, and a baby on the way."

"Don't start crying," Richard said. "We'll think of something."

"What do you want to do about it?" June asked Katie.

"She's planning to have the baby," Neil answered for her.

"I'm really sorry," Katie told them. "I could go away for a while. Genna could run the store for me."

"Yes," June said. "That's exactly what you could do. You've always wanted to see Paris again, and it's high time you had a real vacation. We would find you a nice little apartment, and—"

"How am I going to sue the hell out of Hastings if Katie's in Paris?" Richard demanded. He frowned. "I suppose we could get her affidavit or have her give a deposition."

June was studying Katie. "Are you sure you want to go through with this? You know what it means."

"My baby will be illegitimate," Katie said simply.

"No," Richard said. "I'll see that Hastings marries you the minute he arrives back in the country. He won't have a choice once he's slapped with a paternity suit."

Katie's mouth fell open. "*Marry* him? I don't want to marry Drew."

Richard tapped his fingers on the table impatiently. "It's the only way. I'll see that his child support is so high that he has to work three jobs to pay it."

"I thought you were having him fired," Neil said, sarcasm slipping into his voice. He noted the pain on Katie's face. He was disappointed in how his parents were taking the news.

"Stay out of this, Neil," his father said.

"Did you hear what Katie said, Dad? She doesn't want to marry the bastard."

June held her hankie to her nose. "We're trying to protect her."

"By forcing her to marry someone she never wants to lay eyes on again?"

"Don't you see?" Richard demanded. "We're trying to salvage what's left of her reputation."

Katie gasped.

June dropped her handkerchief into her coffee.

Richard touched his fingers to his forehead as he looked at Katie. "That's not the way I meant it, honey."

"Okay, the two of you have said enough," Neil cut in. His parents looked at him. "Katie has a fine reputation. She has always done what was expected of her. Her only mistake was falling for the wrong guy." He turned to Katie, and his heart wrenched at the sight of her glistening eyes. She was on the verge of breaking down. "You want a name for your baby, kiddo, you got it. I'll give you mine."

June was squeezing coffee from her napkin. "Neil, what are you saying?"

His gaze never left Katie's. "That should be obvious," he said. "I'm asking Katie to marry me."

Four

There was a gasp. Katie didn't realize it had come from her own lips until she felt her breath escape in a gush of hot air. Richard and June stared at their son in utter stupefaction. One would have thought he'd just announced he was joining the Peace Corps and heading to Timbuktu. Katie's head swam. Had she heard right? Had Neil just offered to marry her? *Marry* her? The man who had bad-mouthed matrimony for as long as she could remember?

Katie continued to stare at him. He smiled, but it didn't quite meet his eyes because they were filled with...with what? Pity?

She could almost hear the words. *Poor Katie Jones. No place to go. What to do with her now?* She could not bear that look, especially coming from Neil Logan.

All at once she shoved her chair from the table. "Excuse me," she mumbled, racing from the dining room despite her sore foot. Her pride had just been shattered. The stitches in her heel seemed insignificant. Tears spurted from her eyes, but she managed to find the ladies' room. Inside, two women chatted as one dried her hands and the other applied lipstick. They paused as Katie rushed into a stall, slammed the metal lever in place and burst into tears.

Neil looked at his parents. He felt like shaking them both. "I don't know what the two of you were thinking, but Katie didn't deserve that."

"I know you think I was hard on her," Richard said, "but I was simply trying to help her."

June dabbed her eyes with her napkin. "Your father and I are very upset, Neil. Katie is like a daughter. We saw what her mother went through trying to raise a child alone. It wasn't easy."

"Katie is stronger than you think. She's also educated, and won't have to resort to cleaning toilets for a living. As far as her being alone, I'm not going to let that happen."

"Neil, you can't possibly marry her," June went on. "She's like your own sister. What would people think?"

Neil pushed his chair from the table. "You should know by now that I don't give a damn *what* people think." He made his way from the dining room to the lobby. Where had Katie gone? Her looked out the double glass doors into the parking lot. He spied the door to the ladies' room and didn't hesitate. He shoved the door open and went inside.

"Katie, are you in here?" He glanced at the two ladies at the sinks and nodded. "Pardon me," he said. He checked beneath the door of each stall until he found Katie's shoes. "Okay, kiddo, open the door. We need to talk."

Katie couldn't believe her ears. Neil had actually followed her into the ladies' room. "You obviously took a wrong turn, Neil. The men's room is next door. Besides, I have nothing to say to you *or* your family."

"I'm not responsible for what my family says or does. But I'm trying to help."

Neil glanced over his shoulders. The women were staring, their eyes wide. "Do you mind?" he said. "We'd like a little privacy here."

They jumped when they realized Neil was addressing them. "Of course," one said, taking her friend's hand and leading her out the door.

"You just feel sorry for me."

He gave a snort. "Feel sorry for *you?*"

"That Drew dumped me, and I'm pregnant."

Neil leaned his head against the metal door that separated them. "Katie, my offer of marriage was sincere. You make it impossible for anyone to feel sorry for you. I have never met a stronger, prouder woman in my life. I'm simply offering you a solution. Not because I think you need help supporting or caring for your baby, but because I know how important it is to you to protect him or her from what you went through growing up."

He paused and wiped his forehead. Talking to her was like talking to a concrete wall, and frankly, he was a bit peeved by her response. He was simply trying to help her, do her a favor. Did she think this was easy for him? He was a bachelor, and he preferred it that way. The last thing he needed was to start feeling obligated to a woman who was carrying another man's baby, a woman who was probably still in love with the man. He should have his head examined for offering his help to begin with.

But this wasn't just any woman, Neil reminded himself. This was Katie. The little girl he'd watched grow into a beautiful, independent woman. He heard her sniff from the other side. She was crying. It made him think of another time, when he'd caught her crying in the garden. It had been her seventh birthday, and his parents had planned an extravagant party for her, complete with a clown and two ponies. Nobody had shown up. It had been his mother's hope that Katie could be introduced into polite society and meet the ''right'' children. June Logan hadn't answered the phone for days, thinking her friends had betrayed her. A week later, she'd found the invitations stuffed inside the purse she'd been carrying the day she'd planned to stop by the post office and mail them. She had apologized profusely to Katie, but Neil knew the seven-year-old had suffered over it, feeling as though she weren't good enough for the wealthy crowd. Fourteen years old and self-centered as hell at the time, Neil had found himself wishing he'd been nicer to her.

''Katie, please talk to me,'' he said. ''This is probably the only decent thing I've ever done for you. I know you're looking for true love and happily-ever-after, but you're in a bind, and I think this arrangement could work if you'd let it. You could move into my place until the baby is born. Once you're settled, you could file for a divorce. Hell, I'll even say it was my fault that our marriage soured.''

Katie's heart wrenched as she considered what Neil was offering. True, he was arrogant and bullheaded, and they couldn't be in the same room five minutes without arguing, but she had to respect the man's willingness to help her. And what were her choices? She knew she could support her child; but she was unable to do the one thing that mattered most, give her baby a name. And she had already embarrassed the Logans by racing from the church in her wedding dress, then announcing her pregnancy. The last thing she wanted to do was cause them further distress.

She opened the door. ''You're very kind, Neil,'' she said. ''I don't know what to say.''

''Say yes. Let me do this for you, Katie. Who knows, I may need your help one day.''

Katie's wedding day found her sitting in her old bedroom, sipping her coffee and watching the rain through the window. Fat droplets drizzled down the panes like melted

butter, and the trees shuddered in the wind. A dreary day
for a wedding. The leaden sky matched Katie's mood. An-
nie, the cook who had replaced Cleo, had sent up a silver
tray of pastries, cheeses and various fruits, but Katie had
no appetite.

Katie had spent almost two hours on the phone with
Genna the night before, discussing her fears about the up-
coming marriage.

"You should talk to Neil," Genna had said.

"I haven't seen or heard from him since the day he offered to marry me," Katie told her. "June thought it would
be more appropriate if I stayed here until the wedding."

Now, as Katie faced her wedding day, she couldn't help
but worry. She suspected something had come up for Neil.
He hadn't called...not even to see how she was holding
up. Probably something to do with a case he was working,
she kept telling herself.

If only she could let go of her doubts.

Katie jumped when a knock sounded at the door. June
stepped in, holding a simple white suit and matching heels.
"I knew you'd be too busy to worry about shopping," she
said, holding the dress out for Katie's perusal, "so I picked
up something. I hope you like it. It has an elastic waistband,
so you should be comfortable."

Katie hadn't given much thought to what she would wear
to her own wedding, other than to pluck one of her nicest
dresses from her closet at Neil's, a dove-gray linen coat-
dress. She hadn't discussed it with June because she feared
the woman would ask about the wedding gown. She
touched the white suit. Raw silk. Understated but classy.
"It's beautiful. Thank you for taking care of it." Katie
squeezed her hand before letting go. "I just want you to
know how much I appreciate all you've done. And Neil—"
She paused. "He's being very honorable about the whole
thing."

"Richard and I are proud of him. It has taken some getting used to, but I think it's for the best." She smiled. "I hope you'll be patient with him. He hasn't a clue about being a husband."

It was on the tip of Katie's tongue to remind June that Neil wasn't going to be her *real* husband, but the woman looked so happy that Katie didn't want to spoil it for her.

Neil arrived only minutes before he was to take his place beside Katie in front of Judge Alfred Spears, an old family friend. Right away Katie noticed a difference in his appearance. The lines on either side of his eyes and mouth were more pronounced. He looked deeply troubled. "Are you okay?" she whispered as they stepped in front of the judge. He nodded and smiled, but the look in his eyes said otherwise.

He was having second thoughts, she told herself, wondering how couples managed to walk down the aisle every day without experiencing what she'd been through. Always a bride, never a wife, she thought ruefully.

Katie fretted throughout the ceremony. Perhaps they should call it off. But it was too late to call it off. So she stood beside Neil, a smile frozen to her face, as one photographer snapped pictures and another captured the scene on his camcorder. Genna was by her side, holding a simple gold wedding band that had belonged to June's father and had been sized to fit Neil. Neil held his grandmother's ring.

Katie chanced a look in Neil's direction as the judge spoke. He smelled of soap and aftershave. His navy suit only emphasized his broad shoulders and dark complexion. Had she been a real bride, she would have considered herself quite lucky to win the heart of such a handsome man.

The Logans smiled as Neil and Katie exchanged vows. The housekeeping staff stood at the back of the room, all of them dressed for the occasion. In the next room a catering service waited to serve a champagne brunch for the small wedding party.

"...I now pronounce you man and wife," Judge Spears said, bringing Katie out of her stupor. "Mr. Logan, you may kiss your bride." Katie met Neil's gaze. He smiled at her as he leaned close and placed a chaste kiss on her lips. Lightbulbs flashed. The judge nodded his approval and faced the group of onlookers. "Ladies and gentleman, allow me be the first to introduce to you Mr. and Mrs. Neil Logan."

Katie was only vaguely aware of the applause, of Genna hugging her tightly and June, tears in her eyes, kissing her on the cheek. "My son could not have made a better choice," she said. Although Katie thought it a strange thing to say, she suspected June was playing her part for the benefit of the others. Richard kissed Katie and shook his son's hand as he congratulated them both.

Finally June turned to her guests. "Please join us in the dining room for a celebration brunch," she said, using her best hostess voice.

"I can't stay," Neil blurted. Everyone stopped and looked in his direction.

June looked alarmed. "What do you mean, you can't stay?"

"Something has come up at work, and—"

June turned to her guests. "Everyone, please go into the dining room. Richard, dear, would you please escort Judge Spears inside. We'll join you in just a moment." She waited until the three of them were alone. She shot her son a withering look. "This is your wedding day, Neil."

"It can't be helped." He turned to Katie. "I'm sorry, but it's important." He kissed their cheeks and hurried out.

Katie and June simply looked at each other. It was obvious the older woman was furious. "Well, there goes your new husband. I just wish, for once, this family could have a *normal* wedding.''

Katie wanted to hide beneath a big rock and never come out.

How Katie had managed to sit through the wedding reception without her so-called husband was beyond her, but she almost wept with relief when it was over. Genna had looked embarrassed for her; June and Richard both wore pinched expressions. Katie held her head high and pretended it didn't matter. ''My husband is working on a very serious case and was called away suddenly,'' she told Judge Spears. ''He asks that everyone accept his sincere regrets.''

The judge had nodded. ''Young lady, you're to be commended for marrying a man in law enforcement. It takes a strong woman to live with a man who works long hours and faces danger on a daily basis.''

Katie had thanked him. She didn't allow the tears to fall until she was safely in her car and on her way.

What had she done?

She was *not* as strong as people thought. Her mother's death had devastated her and irrevocably changed her. She feared loss with every cell of her being. To become even temporarily involved with Neil, a man who put his life on the line every time he walked out the door, terrified her.

What had she been thinking?

She had been desperate.

She could *not* think about it right now or she'd go crazy. She had enough to worry about, what with her pregnancy, getting her things from the house she and Drew had planned to share after the wedding and going back to work. She had to get back to the bookstore.

Katie drove straight to the house she and Drew had leased, where she began gathering her clothes from the closets. It was an all-day job. By the time Katie carried in the last load, she was exhausted and her heel throbbed, but she was determined to finish unpacking.

Neil arrived home after nine o'clock and found Katie napping on the sofa. "You look tired. Are you okay?"

She yawned and told him how she'd spent the day. He didn't look pleased. "I would have helped you with that."

"I wanted to get it over with as soon as possible. I feel better knowing my things are here." Besides, she didn't want to impose on him further, and deep down she knew she didn't want to start depending on him. "You don't look so good yourself." The worry lines had deepened. "Is something going on at work?"

"Nothing I can't handle." A look of remorse crossed his face. "I'm sorry for bailing out on you today."

"You showed up for the main attraction. You did your part, and I thank you."

Neil appreciated her understanding, but he wasn't blind to the hurt in her eyes. He wished he could share all that had happened in the past few days, but he didn't feel comfortable discussing it with her, simply because he'd become accustomed to dealing with things on his own. "My mother will never speak to me again."

"She'll get over it."

"How's the foot?"

"Fine." It ached something fierce, but Katie wouldn't complain. She sensed he had something on his mind, and he didn't need to hear about her ailments. She got up from the sofa and made for the kitchen. "How about leftovers tonight?"

"Don't bother to cook. I'll order pizza. What do you like?"

She had never been so thankful for carryout food. "I usually order a vegetarian with half the amount of cheese."

"That's boring, Katie."

"I have to keep my figure."

"You shouldn't diet right now, Katie. You're pregnant."

She didn't answer.

Neil wished he could take back his words. He had no business telling her what she should or shouldn't eat. "Of course, it's up to you," he added quickly.

When the pizza arrived, they ate in silence. Neil couldn't resist watching her. He had never seen anyone eat a slice of pizza so daintily. Katie took small bites and wiped her mouth each time. She would have been appalled to see how he and his partner ate lunch.

Neil glanced at his wristwatch. "I have to go back out," he said, "and I have no idea what time I'll get back."

For the second time that day, Katie tried to keep her disappointment at bay. "You don't have to hang around on my account. I'm turning in early."

He patted her on the shoulder and headed for the door.

Once Katie had wrapped the leftover pizza, she prepared for bed, only to lie awake for an hour, wondering where Neil had gone. She wondered if he was seeing someone, and was surprised how much it bothered her. Then she reminded herself she had no right to feel as she did. Neil was free to see anyone he liked.

Nevertheless, her mind was still troubled as she drifted off to sleep.

Five

One day, the following week, Neil arrived home after work looking better than he had in days. The lines about his eyes and mouth had softened, and he seemed more relaxed. He even teased Katie about her cooking, although he ate everything on his plate.

"There's a solution to that, you know," she replied, relieved that some of his tension had dissipated. "Do your own cooking."

"Hey, I pick up groceries on the way home and clean up the kitchen afterward. That's a lot, considering the mess you make in the kitchen."

"All great chefs make a mess in the kitchen." He opened his mouth to say something, and she shot him a dark look. "Watch it, Logan, or you'll find a TV dinner on the table tomorrow night."

Neil grinned. It felt good to have something to smile about. "Oh, I almost forgot." He pulled something from his shirt pocket and handed it to her. "It's an invitation. Several of the guys at work are throwing us a party Friday night."

Katie couldn't hide her surprise. "Have you told them anything?"

He looked puzzled. "Like what?"

"The truth about our marriage."

"That would be defeating our purpose, wouldn't it? They think it's for real." He paused. "They wanted to throw a bachelor's party for me, but something came up so we had to cancel. I'd like to show up for the party, even if we decide to leave early."

"Then we'll attend, and I'll play the charming, devoted wife."

He chuckled. "You'll have to walk behind me at a respectful distance."

"When pigs fly."

"All the wives do it," he insisted, his eyes bright with amusement, "to honor us as heroes."

Katie was glad to see the old Neil had returned. "Should I bring a pillow so that I can kneel before you, as well?"

"That's not a bad idea. I think it's time someone put women in their place."

Katie knew he was teasing, but she couldn't resist throwing a roll at him. It bounced off his forehead.

He rubbed his noggin. "Hey, that hurt."

"Surely not. A big tough-guy-hero-stud like you."

"I'm not going to lower my standards and get into a food fight with you, Katie." He donned a haughty look and sniffed as though he were way above it.

"You sound just like your mother. Perhaps you should borrow her pearls."

"That does it!" Neil stood, scooped a handful of mashed potatoes with one hand and walked toward her. Katie squealed and jumped from her chair.

"Don't you dare!" she said.

"You've got it coming, Miss Mouth, and you know it."

She darted around the table. Neil stood on the opposite side, waiting. Katie felt like a treed raccoon. "Neil, stop this nonsense right now! All I did was throw a roll."

"Come on, Katie, make your move."

"I'm with child, remember? I'm at a clear disadvantage."

He smiled. "Tell you what, I'm letting you off the hook this time, simply because I'm a nice guy, and I know how much you enjoy soaking in the tub after dinner."

"Yeah, whatever." But she was smiling as she hurried down the hall toward the bathroom. The old Neil was back.

Neil heard the bathwater running as he began clearing the table. He tried not to think of a naked Katie soaking in a tub of bubbles, but his thoughts ran amok nonetheless. He had accidentally seen her nude before, but he'd never told a soul. She'd been seventeen at the time and had just graduated from high school. He'd been twenty-four, on break from the academy. He hadn't been able to sleep that night so he'd decided on a midnight swim, only to pause at the sliding glass door when he saw Katie climbing out, naked as the day she was born.

He should have turned around and gone straight to his bedroom, but he hadn't. He'd watched her from the shadows, wet hair slick against her back, water sluicing down her lithe young body. She was unlike anything he'd ever seen, her breasts perfect globes of alabaster against her tanned skin. She might be on the small side, but everything about her was perfect, her trim waist and softly rounded hips. A behind to die for. Her legs were shapely, swimmer's legs that made a man long to place his body between them and…

Even now Neil remembered how embarrassed he'd felt, unable to pry his eyes off her. Katie was like a sister and still a kid as far as he was concerned. A feeling of shame had forced him to return to his room.

But things had changed.

He'd obviously been too long without a woman. He blamed it on work, his increased caseload, but he knew differently. He simply didn't want to go through the motions. He knew his limits. He enjoyed women, had even enjoyed his share of relationships, but in the end somebody always got hurt because he was only willing to go so far where his emotions were concerned.

The last person he wanted to hurt was Katie.

The last person he should be thinking about in such a way was Katie.

By the time she climbed from her hot bath, Katie felt renewed and invigorated. The hot water had eased the ache in her heel. She towel-dried her hair and fluffed it out so that it fell damp against her shoulders. She powdered herself, taking time to view her tummy sideways in the large mirror over the sink. It was still flat. She wondered what she would look like when it grew large. She stuck it out as far as it would go and frowned. She imagined herself waddling about the bookstore in a maternity outfit and wrinkled her nose at the image. She stepped on the bathroom scale. Lord, Lord, she had gained three pounds!

In her bedroom, Katie donned a pair of satin pajamas and grabbed a pillow from the bed. She stuffed it inside the waistband of her pajama bottoms, pulling her shirt over it. She stepped in front of the mirror, viewing herself from all angles. She looked as big as a bus! She glanced down. Her feet had all but disappeared. She could only make out the tips of her toes, each nail painted a soft rose.

Suddenly, she burst into tears. She crawled onto her bed and plopped a pillow over her face.

Neil tapped lightly on Katie's door and waited. Had she

gone outside? He cracked the door and peeked inside. Both brows arched high on his forehead. "Katie, what the hell are you doing? Katie?"

She bolted upright at the sound of his voice and wiped her eyes with the balls of her hands. Neil stood just outside her door, wearing a perplexed frown. "Have you ever heard of knocking?" she asked.

"I *did* knock. What's going on? Have you been crying?"

Katie leaped to her feet. "Look at me, Neil," she said, pointing to the pillow beneath her shirt. "This is what I'm going to look like before long." She gave him a side view. "I look like I just swallowed an ice-cream truck."

He nodded. Actually, she looked downright adorable, but he knew he'd never convince her. "I wouldn't count on a date for the prom," he said instead.

Katie pulled the pillow from her pajamas and threw it at him. He ducked. "Hey, there'll be no more throwing things," he said sternly, even as he looked as though he would burst into laughter. "And stop crying. It's just your hormones acting up."

She looked at him. "How do you know?"

"The guys at work have wives. They've all gone through it. When is your next doctor's appointment?"

"In a couple of weeks."

"You need to discuss these little...mood swings."

She wasn't listening. "From now on, I'm on a diet. If I get too big, I'll have stretch marks. And what if I retain water? My feet will be the size of cantaloupes, and my fingers will look like link sausages."

"You're right. You're going to look disgusting." He shuddered.

She glared at him. "Did you want something in particular?"

"Yeah. You want to go with me to the Dairy Queen?"

"I'm in my pajamas."

"We'll order at the drive-through window. Nobody will see you."

Katie grabbed a knee-length raincoat with polka dots from her closet and slipped into bedroom shoes that were so furry it looked as though an oversize cat had planted itself on each foot. "I'm ready."

Neil stifled the urge to laugh as they walked out to his Jeep. He unlocked her door and opened it. Once he joined her in the front seat he found her looking at him strangely. "What?"

"You don't have to open the door for me. We're not on a date."

"I always open the door for a lady. My father drilled it into me as I was growing up."

"This is different."

"Fine. Next time I'll just start down the road, and you can grab on to the bumper. How about that?"

"You're being disagreeable."

"You're making a big deal out of nothing."

"I'm just trying to set things straight in the beginning, so you won't have to go to any extra trouble. I don't want to interfere with your life. As a matter of fact, I want you to pretend I'm not even around."

"That won't be easy. The house already smells like you."

She looked at him. "Are you saying I have an odor?"

Neil sighed. "I'm saying everyone has a certain scent. How do you think our K9 Unit tracks missing persons? You have a feminine scent. It's nice."

"It is?"

"It's not overwhelming, just a light scent."

He pulled into the Dairy Queen and stopped beside a metal box, where a voice took their order. Katie gave very specific directions as to how she wanted her ice cream.

When they pulled away a few minutes later, Neil couldn't help but shoot side glances at her.

She stopped licking her ice cream. "What?"

"You've sort of blown your diet, haven't you?"

She blushed at the size of her ice cream-cone. She'd ordered the large, topped with chocolate and nuts. "I'll eat light tomorrow."

Katie was still licking her ice cream when they arrived home. "I'm going to drop you off, if you don't mind. I need to run out for a little while."

"Now?"

"Yeah. I won't be gone long. Don't forget to lock up."

Katie felt her mouth droop. And here they'd been having so much fun. She let herself out of the Jeep. "Thanks for the ice-cream cone."

Neil waited until she was safely inside before he pulled away.

Neil pulled into the hospital parking lot twenty minutes later and found a parking spot right away. Visiting hours were over, but the doctors and nursing staff had made allowances for him. If Jim Henderson, his partner, was sedated, at least he could visit with the man's family for a few minutes and see how he was doing. His partner had been shot two days before his wedding to Katie.

The lobby was deserted except for a gray-haired lady at the information desk, who smiled at Neil in recognition. He smiled back and headed toward the elevators. In the visitor's lounge he found Jim's wife, Teresa, sitting beside the man's mother, both of them thumbing through magazines in such a way it was obvious they weren't interested in the articles inside. They smiled when they spotted Neil.

"How is he?"

Teresa stood and hugged Neil. "He was in pain so they gave him something. He's sleeping now. Actually, we were about to leave. Why don't you go home and get some shut-eye? You look like you could use some."

"I won't be long." Neil looked in on Jim briefly. He hated seeing the man as he looked now, tubes everywhere, machines lit up all around, making soft bleeping noises. Jim had lost a lot of blood, and although Neil had stood in line with the family to donate his own, he wished he could do more. The good news was that Jim had been moved from intensive care, and his condition was no longer critical.

Finally Neil joined the two women who were waiting just outside the door as though they were trying to afford Neil a private moment with his friend.

"He looks better, don't you think?" Teresa said. "Some of his color has returned."

Neil nodded. Jim *did* look somewhat better, but he still had a long way to go. "Let me walk you ladies to your car," he said. "Two good-looking women like yourselves shouldn't be out alone this time of night."

Teresa shook her head. "Always on duty, aren't you, Logan?"

He waited until they were safely locked inside Teresa's car before he headed in the direction of his Jeep. He sat there for a moment. He was in no hurry to return home in case Katie was still awake. He had seen the questions in her eyes, and he wasn't ready to answer them. He was trying to act as if everything was fine. The woman had enough worries without him adding to them. He needed time to think, time to sort through his feelings. He had learned the hard way that he couldn't bury them deep inside or he would self-destruct.

He drove to a sports bar, chose a booth in the back and ordered a beer.

He had never felt so weary. He wished he could relive the day Jim was shot, wished he had acted more quickly, preventing his partner from taking that near-fatal bullet. He was the chief detective, and Jim had only recently been promoted. Jim lacked Neil's experience, even though he'd worked the streets years before becoming a detective.

Neil played the pictures through his mind, as he'd done a hundred times since the incident occurred. He and Jim had been investigating a neighborhood once rife with drugs and prostitution, a neighborhood where mothers had kept their children inside because gang members roamed the streets freely and homicides occurred on a regular basis.

Neil had decided long ago to clean it up. He liked to think his efforts were paying off. The APD had busted more hookers and drug dealers than they had room to hold, and it was ongoing because Captain Burns sent cruisers through on a regular basis. Neil was a hero as far as the law-abiding citizens in the area went, setting up a neighborhood watch program and enlisting the help of other agencies. An old building had been torn down, and the owner had turned it into a park, erecting a five foot tall concrete block wall around it for added safety.

Neil and Jim had been standing inside, watching a group of teenagers shoot hoops and giving them a hard time, as usual, and the boys were giving as good as they got. Nearby, an elderly woman pushed a child on a swing.

The sound came from out of nowhere, a fast-running engine, the screech of tires as a car careened around the corner, music blaring from speakers that had never been designed to go into an auto. Neil ordered the teenagers to hit the ground as he raced for the child in the swing, Jim on his heels. The grandmother, obviously hard of hearing, had simply stood there, looking confused.

Everything happened quickly: the sound of gunfire, the boy screaming in fear as Neil yanked him from the swing and threw himself across his small body. And Jim, running toward the elderly woman who still didn't seem to know what was going on.

Jim and the grandmother were a split second too late.

The grandmother had not made it.

The teenagers had tried to keep the little boy occupied while Neil performed CPR on Jim as he prayed for the ambulance to arrive.

What could he have done differently? Neil wondered, even now. What could he have done to prevent it?

He suspected the hit had been meant for him. He might be well liked by those who wanted a safe place to live, but there were others who hated the APD—Neil Logan, specifically, for taking over their territory. Neil had it from a good source that a major drug dealer still lived in the vicinity, a man who was suspected of ordering hits to certain dealers who'd tried to cheat him.

The shooters had simply aimed at the wrong cop. A heavy burden to carry.

Neil suddenly thought of Ryan, his best friend, now dead fifteen years. Neil hadn't been able to prevent that tragedy either, and it still ate at him.

He wondered if other people had demons.

"Dammit to hell," he muttered under his breath, and drained his beer. He left the bar because he knew his thoughts were treading on dangerous ground. He would do his best to find the damn car, *and* the men who'd gunned down two people, and when he did there would be hell to pay.

He stopped in his tracks. Finding the shooters wasn't enough. He had to find the man behind it all.

On Friday Katie fussed in front of the bathroom mirror for more than an hour before trying on three different outfits. She wanted to look especially nice for the party Neil's co-workers were throwing for them, and although he'd told her everyone would dress casually, she still fretted. She finally decided on navy slacks and a lightweight sweater of navy and white. The waistband of the slacks felt snug. Katie wondered if it was just her imagination because she knew she was pregnant. As she exited the room, she found Neil sitting in front of the TV watching the news, Bruno at his feet.

He looked up and smiled. "You look pretty." Bruno thumped his tail against the wood floor. "See, Bruno thinks so, too." He punched the remote, and the TV screen went black.

Katie couldn't help feeling a bit nervous. They were going out together as man and wife. It wasn't as simple as jumping into his Jeep in her bathrobe and driving to the Dairy Queen for ice cream. It was important that she make a good impression on his friends.

"You look nice, too," she said, noting his starched khaki slacks and a rugby shirt that matched his eyes. Yep, Neil Logan was a handsome devil, and he knew it.

He stood, gazed down at her. "You're nervous."

"No."

"Yes. You gnaw on the inside of your bottom lip when you get nervous. You're doing it now."

She should have known she couldn't fool him. "Okay, I'm a little anxious."

"Just be yourself."

"I can't be myself. I'm supposed to be your wife. I don't know how a wife is supposed to act."

He shrugged as he opened her car door. "Just act like you adore me and can't keep your hands off me."

"When hell freezes over."

"Aw, Katie, admit it. You're hot for me."

He was grinning. She gave him one of her looks. "Time for a reality check, Logan."

"You know what your problem is, Miss Jones? You're

a perfectionist. Everything has to be *just so*. Just like my mother,'' he added, frowning slightly. ''Oh, Lord, I've gone and married my mother.''

Katie chuckled as he started the engine and pulled out of the driveway. ''I consider that a compliment.''

''There's such a thing as going too far. Your makeup and hair don't have to be perfect every minute of the day.'' As if to prove his point, Neil reached over and mussed her hair.

Katie shrieked. ''Why did you do that?'' She flipped the visor down, and, using the mirror as her guide, finger-combed her hair into place.

''You need to chill out, Katie, or you'll drive me crazy long before the baby comes.''

''Oh, yeah? Well, take this!'' She reached over and ruffled her fingers through his hair.

Neil merely smiled as he glanced into the rearview mirror, then at Katie, who looked proud of herself. ''You think that's funny?''

''Yep. You look like you just climbed out of bed.''

''Great. I'm going to leave it like this.''

She looked at him. ''Why?''

''That's how a newly married man *should* look. Like he just climbed out of bed with his bride. I think I should go in with my pants unzipped, as well.''

Katie blushed. Neil was getting frisky on her, and she didn't quite know how to respond, but she certainly didn't need to walk around thinking of what lay behind his zipper! ''You're going to comb your hair before we go in, Neil Logan, or I'm not going in with you.''

''I don't have a comb.''

She pulled one from her purse. ''I do.''

''I'm not combing it, Katie. I want the guys to think I'm getting laid on a regular basis now.''

This time she gawked. ''Neil, you are incorrigible, and

I'm not about to set foot in some stranger's house with your hair looking like that. *I'll* comb it.'' She unlocked her seat belt, twisted around in the seat and began combing his thick hair into place. Why did it have to feel so good between her fingers?

"Hey, you're supposed to be wearing a seat belt, young lady. Don't make me stop the car and arrest you.'' He paused. "On second thought, you might look good in handcuffs.''

She rolled her eyes heavenward. Lord, Lord, what had gotten into the man? "I'm not scared of you, Logan.'' All she could do was try to act casual about his risqué remarks. No way was she about to let him think he was getting to her.

Neil sat still as Katie put his hair in order. He liked the feel of her fingers touching his scalp, causing it to prickle. The hairs on the back of his neck stood on end, and he felt certain stirrings he knew he had no business feeling. Just from her combing his hair! Heaven only knew what would happen if she gave him a haircut. One thing for sure, he wouldn't risk it while sitting behind the wheel of his Jeep. She smoothed the back of his hair down, and her fingers brushed his neck. His gut tightened. Had she been anyone but Katie, he would have turned the Jeep around, taken her home and shown her just what she was doing to him.

Neil pulled into a neat subdivision and slowed in front of a brick house where colorful mums adorned the flowerbeds. Cars lined the block. He glanced about, wondering where they would park.

"Whose house is this?'' Katie asked.

He hesitated. "Dave Sanders.''

Katie gaped at him. "Not the same man—''

"Yes.''

"What did you tell him?''

"I simply said you'd broken off your wedding the day before our little mishap in the alley, because you realized you were madly in love with me, which is understandable considering how handsome I am. Told him we decided to marry right away. You want me to just drop you off here? I'm going to have to park in that cul-de-sac at the end of the street."

"No, I'll walk. I need all the exercise I can get. Didn't Dave question why I was sitting in a pile of refuse in an alley, wearing a gown that cost more than most mobile homes?" she asked, resuming their conversation.

Neil pulled up beside the curb at the end of the street and parked. "I told him it was a long story. Besides, I think he was more interested in trying to figure out why a good-looking guy like me would marry a shrimp of a woman like yourself."

"I'm *not* a shrimp."

He gave a snort. "You're a runt. You make short people look tall. Not to mention a sissy."

She was fast becoming indignant. "I am definitely *not* a sissy."

"I've seen your bathroom, kiddo. You've got enough soaps and bubble bath in there to open your own store. You fog the whole house when you get into that fancy powder you wear." He wasn't about to mention the panties and bras drying on the towel racks. *If* they could be called panties. There wasn't enough material in them to clothe a moth.

"I like nice smells."

"Which explains why we have fifty scented candles in the house. Sit tight, I'll get your door."

"I can do it." She reached for the handle.

"Don't be disagreeable." He opened the door and climbed out.

Katie sighed. This wasn't going to be easy.

Neil helped her out a moment later. "Now, remember, try to stay as close to the truth as you can."

"And pretend I can't take my eyes off you," she mumbled, following the octagon-shaped stepping-stones that led to the front door.

"That's the easy part, babe. What's not to like?" Neil smacked her lightly on the behind and rang the doorbell. He gave a mental flinch when Katie jerked her head around and gaped at him. Now, what had gone and made him do *that,* he wondered. He'd acted strictly on impulse, but he had no right to touch her that way. "Sorry," he mumbled as the door was thrown open.

Dave greeted them. "Here they are, folks," he called out over his shoulder. "The bride and groom have arrived!"

Katie forced a smile to her face. She couldn't think about the smack on her behind that Neil had just delivered. He had never touched her intimately, but he obviously hadn't been thinking, and the last thing she needed to do was overreact.

Instead, she stepped inside the Sanders' home prepared to give the acting job of her life.

Six

Marjorie Sanders rushed forward and hugged Katie tightly. She was a slender brunette, taller than her husband by a couple of inches. "Welcome to the family, honey. Dave said you were pretty, but I had no idea just how much."

"You look different from the last time I saw you," Dave said, patting Katie's hand. When she blushed, he winked. "Please allow me to kiss the bride." He grabbed her, made a production of leaning her way back in his arms and planting a kiss on her mouth.

"Easy, Dave," a man said, stepping forward. "She's a newlywed. Neil will kill you if you cause her to throw her back out." Those in the background laughed.

"This is Archer Burns, our captain," Neil said, "and this gorgeous woman with him is Betty."

Katie shook both of their hands. Dave led them inside and began making introductions, although Katie was certain she would never remember everybody's name. The only thing she was conscious of at that moment was Neil's arm around her. He was holding her close, so close she could feel the heat from his body, his hard thighs against hers. His scent enveloped her, and she half feared she would become dizzy.

"What'll you have to drink?" Dave asked.

Katie had trouble finding her tongue.

Neil dropped a kiss on the top of her head. He could tell she was a bit flustered at all the attention, and he pulled her closer, feeling a sense of protectiveness toward her. "A diet soft drink for my beautiful wife, and I'll take a cold beer if you have one."

Marjorie chuckled. "We've always got cold beer." She glanced at her husband before making her way into the kitchen. "Dave, point them in the direction of the food. Neil, wipe that lovesick grin off your face, and for Pete's sake let go of your poor wife so she can get something to eat."

Katie glanced up at Neil quickly. *Lovesick grin?* Well, he *was* grinning from ear to ear, but it was all part of the act. Suddenly she realized she was grinning, as well, and she had to admit it felt good to be around people again after having spent the past week hiding out at Neil's. That wasn't the only reason she was grinning, though, but she wasn't about to admit it had anything to do with being Neil's date for the evening.

Neil introduced Katie to several others who were already gathered around the table, filling their plates. An assortment of platters contained sandwich meats, various cheeses, vegetable trays, spicy chicken and teriyaki wings. A woman named Sally carried in a plate piled high with nachos and all the fixings. "Be careful," she warned, "it just came out of the oven."

Neil turned his head slightly so that his mouth was at Katie's ear once again. "You okay?"

She nodded, despite the fact her insides were jangling and she was weak-kneed from standing so close to him. Neil Logan made her feel more feminine. He'd teased her about being a sissy, but there was something about his maleness that brought out her softer side, a vulnerability that she'd tried to cover with strength and independence. Strange that she was just now realizing these things.

Marjorie appeared with their drinks. "Everything smells and looks delicious," Katie told her. "Neil and I appreciate your going to all this trouble."

Marjorie waved the statement aside. "Oh, it was nothing. Everybody pitched in."

As Katie prepared her plate, she wondered what Neil's mother would make of the spread. June Logan would never have asked friends to bring food to one of her parties. She would have called a catering service and insisted on using her finest china and silver. She would never have permitted a chicken wing or a cocktail weenie on her table, nor would she run back and forth to her kitchen for soft drinks and beer when it would have been easier to hire a bartender to serve only the finest wine and liquor. But this friendly gathering of couples, wives who'd spent hours in their own kitchens cooking for Neil and Katie's wedding party, meant more to her than a fancy seven-course meal.

Neil stayed by Katie's side, laughing at the ribald comments some of the couples made. "Don't let them embarrass you," he whispered, his mouth touching Katie's ear. "They're just having fun."

She shivered at his touch, his lips on her outer ear, his breath warm on her cheek. "I know."

Once they'd eaten their fill, Katie carried her plate and Neil's to the kitchen where she found Marjorie rinsing dishes and putting them into the dishwasher. "This was so kind of everybody," Katie said.

"Don't be silly," the woman replied, taking the plates

from her. "We were all dying to meet Neil's new wife and welcome you into the fold. Frankly, we all wanted to box his ears when he gave us the news *after* the wedding, but I wasn't all that surprised since Neil is such a private person."

"It all happened so quickly," Katie said.

Marjorie smiled. "I read the society column, honey."

Katie blushed. "Then you know about the fiasco I created," she said, her voice deadpan.

"I'm just thankful you and Neil realized you were in love before you walked down the aisle with the wrong man. It's obvious the two of you are crazy about each other."

"It is?" In Katie's surprise, the words slipped out uncensored.

"Well, of course, honey. I've never seen Neil so happy. I'm just sorry his partner and wife aren't here to meet you. You'll love Jim and Teresa Henderson."

"I hope to meet them soon."

Marjorie shook her head. "I don't expect Jim to be out of the hospital anytime soon."

"Is he ill?"

Marjorie gave her a funny look. "Didn't Neil tell you?"

Katie's own look was blank. "Tell me what?"

"Jim was shot in the stomach last week. I'm surprised you didn't read about it in the newspaper or see it on the news. A drive-by shooting by a couple of hoodlums high on crack. Neil saved a little boy's life, but his grandmother was killed, and Jim was hit. Happened a couple of days before your wedding."

The color drained from Katie's face. Now she understood why Neil hadn't contacted her before the wedding and why he'd rushed off afterward. Why he was late coming home and why he often went back out. The mood swings. And here she'd thought he was seeing someone. She was ashamed of herself. "I'm so sorry to hear it," she managed.

"Well, Neil probably didn't want to upset you with it, what with the two of you getting married and all, but I know the poor guy has been worried sick. You know how Neil is, he keeps things to himself and pretends everything is fine. I hear he visits the hospital several times a day. Neil suspects the bullet was meant for him."

Katie looked up sharply. "Why?"

"Cops make enemies. Especially the tough ones."

"How is Jim?" Katie asked, wanting to change the subject.

Marjorie's smile faded slightly. "His condition was critical at first, of course, but he has stabilized. But Teresa, bless her heart, is trying so hard to be strong for him. It can't be easy, what with three little ones to care for and her working full-time. Fortunately, their families are very supportive and they live close by."

"I'm so very sorry," Katie repeated.

Marjorie closed the dishwasher and regarded her. "I wish I hadn't told you. I just assumed Neil had." When Katie didn't respond, she went on. "It's part of being a cop's wife, honey. Please don't say anything to Neil. We all agreed not to discuss Jim tonight and spoil your wedding celebration. I'm sure Neil will tell you in his own time."

Katie tried not to let the woman know just how upset she was over the news. She remembered how hard it had been on Neil when his best friend, Ryan, died, how the family feared he would never get over it. Neil had blamed himself.

Neil came into the kitchen at just that moment. He noted the look on Katie's face. "Is something wrong, honey?"

She smiled at the endearment. He had been so attentive all evening that it was hard to remember he was just playing a role. He was enjoying being with his friends, and she wouldn't do or say anything to put a damper on the evening. "I was just thanking Marjorie for going to so much trouble for us."

"Don't get carried away," he said. "She and Dave owe me."

Marjorie shot him a dirty look. "You're never going to let me off the hook, are you?" She looked at Katie. "Neil helped Dave and me paint this house from top to bottom when we bought it. We've been indebted to him ever since."

"Tell her *when* I helped paint the house, Marjorie."

She rolled her eyes. "Superbowl Sunday."

Katie laughed. "You're right. He'll never let you off the hook."

Katie and Neil exchanged looks, and she saw the warmth in his eyes. Why hadn't he told her about his partner? She tried not to let her disappointment show. After all, she wasn't his real wife, and they had pretty much agreed to go on with their lives as before. Nevertheless, she was hurt that he hadn't shared his troubles. Heaven knew she'd shared hers.

Dave stepped just inside the kitchen. "We need y'all in the living room." He motioned them to follow.

Katie shot a questioning look at Marjorie, but the woman merely shrugged. As they walked into the living room, Katie saw that everyone seemed to be waiting. Archer Burns, the captain, stood in the center, an envelope in his hand.

"Aw, there they are. Come on over here, kids." He waited until Neil and Katie were by his side. He made a production of clearing his throat. "We were thrilled to hear about your nuptials. But it was all so quick none of us had time to go out and shop for wedding presents. Instead, we all chipped in fifty cents apiece and bought you and your wife a gift certificate from Saks. I don't know what you can buy at Saks for less than twenty-five bucks, but, hey, it's the thought that counts." Burns handed Neil the envelope, and he passed it to Katie.

Katie opened it. Inside was a nice card congratulating them on their wedding, and a five-hundred-dollar gift certificate to Saks Fifth Avenue. She smiled shyly at the group. "Thank you very much," she said as she passed it to Neil. He echoed her sentiments, and there was more clapping. Katie heard the sound of popping corks and saw Marjorie, Dave and several others pouring champagne into disposable champagne glasses.

"I see our host and hostess are getting out the bubbly so, while we're waiting, I'll say a few words," Burns said, only to be met with groans from the onlookers. He ignored them and faced Katie. His look softened. "Katie, honey, it's not always easy being a cop's wife. My own wife will tell you that. Sometimes the hours are long. Especially at night," he added, glancing at his wife, who offered him a thoughtful smile, "and there have been some long nights in our marriage when I know Betty worried about me and wished she'd married a plumber so she could live in high style." Several people chuckled. "Seems plumbers are the ones making all the money these days," Burns added.

He paused when Marjorie carried over a tray of champagne glasses and waited for them each to take one. "Anyway, we all hope you and Neil don't have too many sleepless nights, and that you'll enjoy becoming part of our family, because that's what we are, really, just one big family." He glanced around as if to see that everyone held a glass. "Neil, Katie—" he held his glass high to toast them "—please accept our sincere congratulations on your marriage, and may you have many happy years together."

Katie felt the moisture building in her eyes as the group toasted them. She tasted her champagne.

"Kiss her, Logan," someone called out from the crowd. Neil leaned toward Katie and kissed her lightly on the lips.

"Man, don't kiss her like she's your mother," another voice said. "Make it good."

Neil met Katie's gaze. His look was playful, pure mirth.

She shrugged and, bolstered by the crowed, tossed him a challenging look. Finally he took her glass and handed it to Archer Burns. He handed his own to Marjorie. Grinning, he shoved his sleeves high on his arms and made a production of squaring his shoulders and dusting off his hands.

"Okay, everybody stand back and take notes," he said, flexing his fingers, "and I'll show you how a pro works." More laughter from the crowd. Neil slipped his arms around Katie, pulled her hard against him and kissed her soundly on the lips.

Surprised, Katie's mouth opened slightly, and Neil slipped his tongue inside, pulling her even closer. She was only vaguely aware of the clapping and wolf whistles as Neil's arms tightened around her.

Their tongues met for the first time.

Katie felt her knees turn to pudding. She grasped Neil's arms for support.

Neil almost groaned out loud when he tasted the sweetness past Katie's lips. Something inside him snapped, and his body came to life. His gut clenched, the muscles in his thighs tensed and he was gripped by a powerful desire to keep right on kissing her. A woman had no right to taste that nice, he told himself.

Katie's head swam, and every one of her senses leaped to life. Her skin prickled and warmed, nerve endings tingled along her spine. Lord, Lord, she thought, what was happening to her?

All at once, and to everyone's pleasure, Neil swooped Katie high in his arms, never once breaking the kiss. He wanted it to last forever. The crowd cheered.

Archer Burns cleared his throat. "Time to come up for air, Logan," he said.

Neil raised his head. He and Katie made eye contact. It was as if he were seeing her for the first time. From the look on her face, he knew she felt it, too. He lowered her to the ground.

"Now that's what I call a kiss," Marjorie said, fanning herself with one hand.

Katie was thankful when Neil announced they were leaving. Marjorie pulled her aside. "You'll have to go out to lunch with us wives sometimes," she said. "We try to get together at least once a month. I don't know if we'll do it this month because we're taking turns cooking and baby-sitting for Teresa."

"Is there anything I can do?" Katie asked.

"We're okay for now, but thanks for asking." Marjorie hugged her. "It was nice meeting you, honey."

Neil noticed Katie was quiet on the ride home. "Did you have a good time?" he asked.

She looked at him. "Oh, yes. Your friends are wonderful, and I especially liked Marjorie."

"I'm glad. You made a good impression. Everybody liked you."

"Just doing my job, Logan."

Her job. He wished she wouldn't keep reminding him. Neil drove a distance. "I hope I didn't embarrass you back there, kissing you like I did. It's just…everybody seemed to expect it, us being newlyweds and all."

Katie didn't want to think about that kiss or the pat on the rump before going in. Somehow, she felt as though it had changed things. "It was all in good fun. Let's just drop it."

All in good fun. Let's just drop it. Which was Katie's way of telling him not to make a big deal out of it. Neil wondered if she knew just what that kiss had done to him. Obviously, it hadn't meant as much to her, and for some reason that didn't sit well with him. *What the hell did you expect, Logan?* They were playing a role. If he'd gotten carried away, it was his own damn fault.

He was falling for her hard and fast, simply because he had gone so long without the soft side of life she represented. But Katie Jones did not belong to him. They were worlds apart, and he'd known it from the beginning. She wanted a home and family; he was a man who would not take the risks.

He'd let down his guard, but he wouldn't make that mistake again.

Sleep did not come easily for Katie. She turned on her lamp and tried to get interested in a book, but her thoughts wouldn't leave her alone. She kept thinking about the Henderson family and wondered how the children were taking the news of their father's injury. She recalled Marjorie's words about being a cop's wife. What if Neil had been hit and was lying in the hospital seriously injured or worse? How would she have handled it? She had known him all her life, had watched him grow up. She had even hated him at times and remembered being thankful when, because of his behavior at school, he was sent to a military school.

She had watched Neil suffer when he'd lost his best friend, who'd climbed behind the wheel of a car one night after having too much to drink. Although Neil hadn't been seriously injured, he had fallen into a depression so deep that doctors feared he would never recover. When Neil *had* finally come out of his depression and recovered physically, he'd surprised his parents and joined the police academy.

His father had been none too happy about his son's decisions. After all, he'd planned for Neil to take over the century-old family magazine. But Neil was determined, and he was obviously good at what he did, since he'd made detective at such an early age. He had received one commendation after another.

Still, Katie wondered if it was enough, wondered if Neil was trying to repay a debt that had not been his fault to begin with. He had changed. On the outside, he appeared cocksure and carefree, but Katie had slowly watched him build a wall around himself that nobody could penetrate. She suspected it was the reason his relationships never lasted.

She was suddenly hit with the knowledge. Neil Logan was just as afraid of loss as she was.

Katie sat bolt upright in the bed as soon as the thought came to mind. She could not imagine Neil being afraid of anything. He had always taken chances, pushed the envelope, so to speak. He was the hellion, the rebel, strong-willed and determined to have his own way. He was the one who refused to cry when it was time to return to military school after the holidays, even though Katie knew he would have given anything to stay home with his family.

It was uncanny just how alike she and Neil were. She had accepted Drew's marriage proposal, knowing deep in her heart she didn't love him as a woman should love the man she was about to marry. Sure, she was comfortable and enjoyed being with him, but she had not wholly given herself to him. His kisses were nice, but her body did not react as it had tonight when Neil had kissed her. She had saved that part of herself, that region of her heart that had been so badly wounded when her mother had died. She had emotionally locked away the most important part of her, her very soul.

Had Drew suspected? Could it be that he had not been willing to settle for less, despite the doors his new father-in-law-to-be could have opened for him?

Katie suddenly saw her ex-fiancé in a whole new light, and she almost didn't blame him for running away. What man wanted to share his life with a woman who refused to get too close? Was she incapable of love? She pressed her hand against her stomach. Would she be incapable of loving her child, too?

Katie's eyes welled up with tears, and she reached for a tissue. Could it be that she and Neil were destined to spend their lives alone because the past had made them fearful?

Marjorie called Katie the following morning. Neil had already left for work; in fact, he was gone when Katie stumbled from her bedroom for a cup of sugar-free cappuccino with extra cream. "Everyone loved you," the woman announced from the other end of the line. "You were a big hit with the captain, as well."

"I'm glad," Katie replied, having wanted so desperately to make a good impression. "I enjoyed meeting everyone, and Neil and I are both deeply touched by the wedding gift."

"It was the least we could do. Everyone loves Neil." She laughed. "I doubt you'll be able to afford your china with five hundred dollars, but you may be able to stock up on towels. You can never have too many towels."

Katie chuckled. "How is Jim Henderson this morning?"

"I haven't spoken with his wife this morning. I plan to call in a little while."

"Is there something I can do?"

Marjorie paused. "Well, if you're serious about helping out, the person who was supposed to cook dinner tonight had to work a double shift."

"I plan on going by the grocery store. I'll pick up fried chicken and all the fixings and drop it off on my way home. Will that be okay?"

"The kids will love it."

An hour later Katie pushed her cart through the supermarket, buying groceries for Neil and her and picking up extra items she thought the Henderson family might need. Once again she wondered how the children were handling their father's injury, but she refused to dwell on it because it would only depress her and because she would start worrying about Neil, his job and their relationship. She had done enough crying the night before, and although she suspected her hormones had a lot to do with it, Neil played a big part. She had decided it best not to ask questions about what he did all day—if he wanted to share routine information, that was fine—but she didn't want to know about the dangerous side of his work. Not that Neil shared it with her, anyway.

Still, she fretted.

It's part of being a cop's wife, honey.

Katie finished her shopping and drove to the Sanders home with the food items. Marjorie looked happy to see her. "Can you join me for a cup of coffee?" she asked. "It's decaffeinated."

"A quick one," Katie replied. "I have groceries in the car." She had intentionally steered clear of the ice-cream section, so she didn't have to worry about it melting in her trunk. Besides, she looked forward to sitting down for a minute. Her heel ached, and she felt unusually tired. As she sipped her coffee, Marjorie filled her in on Jim's condition, which had taken another turn for the better.

"Jim and Teresa's church has been great," Marjorie said, "holding garage sales and pancake and spaghetti dinners. They've prompted other churches to become involved." The woman paused. "By the way, has Neil said anything yet?"

Katie shook her head. "Not a word."

"These guys take it hard when a partner is injured. Or worse." Marjorie glanced away.

Katie made no reply. She didn't want to think about it. Instead she stretched. "I'm so tired. I think all this wedding business has taken a toll on me because all I want to do is sleep.''

''Maybe you're pregnant.''

Katie almost choked on her coffee. Her face suddenly felt hot.

''You're blushing, Katie. Profusely, I might add.''

''Oh, well, I—'' She tried to think of a response, but her tongue wouldn't cooperate.

Marjorie shot her a speculative look. ''Are you?''

Katie looked down at the toes of her sneakers. ''Yes.''

''How far along?''

''Three months. Please don't say anything to anyone.''

''I figure it's yours and Neil's business, and I'm not one to reveal confidences. What you say here, stays here.'' She studied Katie. ''You don't appear to be very excited about it.''

For some reason Katie trusted the woman, although she'd known her less than twenty-four hours. And Neil trusted her, or so it seemed. That had to mean something.

Marjorie patted her hand. ''Listen, I was pregnant when I married Dave. Nobody suspected a thing. People really don't pay attention to that sort of thing these days, except old ladies who don't have anything better to do. So stop worrying. Even the old ladies will be thrilled once they see the baby and how much Neil loves you.''

Katie saw the concern in Marjorie's eyes, and she suspected they would be friends long after she and Neil went their separate ways. ''Marjorie, I think I should tell you the truth.''

Seven

Katie returned to work the following Monday to a surprise party given by Genna. Doris, who worked the food counter and made the best gourmet coffee and specialty sandwiches Katie had ever tasted, had hung white paper wedding bells in the cozy eating area and tied two dozen white and silver helium balloons to the backs of the chairs. Almost twenty of Katie's frequent customers had shown up for the event, each carrying a wedding gift.

Katie was touched, first by Genna and Doris's thoughtfulness, and by her customers for caring enough to share the occasion. If only her marriage weren't a ruse. Then she wouldn't have to feel so guilty accepting everyone's congratulations.

"You guys outdid yourselves," she told Genna and Doris before the lunch crowd arrived. "I can't thank you enough." They barely had time to clean up before the eating area filled with the usual lunch crowd. Although her employees had managed wonderfully in her absence, Katie was glad to be back.

The day passed quickly. Doris left precisely at five so she could relieve the sitter who kept her children after school until she arrived home from work. Once Genna put up the Closed sign, she slumped in a wicker settee that had been placed in the bay window to give the store a homey look. She gave a sigh of relief. "Busy day," she said.

Katie joined her, kicking off her low pumps. Her heel throbbed, despite the extra padding she'd put in her shoes. Although she'd had the stitches removed and the wound was healing wonderfully, it had flared up after standing on her feet all day. She propped them on the small wicker coffee table. "Very busy," she agreed. "I'd forgotten how much running we do around here."

"So, when is your next doctor's visit?"

"This Friday at 3:00 p.m. I'll have to leave early."

Genna nodded. "How are things at the ranch? Are you and Neil getting along okay?"

"Actually, we're doing very well. I never thought it would work. Of course, it's still early. We might be going for each other's throats by the end of the month."

"People change, Katie. The two of you have grown up. Neil seems very fond of you. You never know what the future might hold."

Katie shook her head. "No way, Genna. I'm not about to let myself fall for a guy who risks his neck every time he leaves for work." She told him about Neil's partner.

"It could have happened to anyone," her friend pointed out.

"True, but Neil's job places him in danger every day. If I ever marry for real, it won't be to a homicide detective. I want a nice stable life for my child."

"Marry a businessman," Genna said. "One who sits at a desk all day and battles stress on a regular basis. The only thing you'll have to worry about is him suffering high blood pressure, a stroke or a heart attack.''

Katie looked at her friend. ''You're not being very helpful.''

''I'm being honest. Love isn't perfect, Katie, although I think that's what you're looking for since you're a perfectionist. Drew Hastings *looked* perfect, what with his cushy job and expensive suits, not to mention that snazzy BMW he drove. But you didn't really love him. You loved the idea of having your own family.''

Katie shook her head. ''You know, sometimes I think you know me better than I know myself.''

''We've been friends for how many years now? You get to know someone pretty well in that length of time.''

Katie stayed busy with work all week. She saw Neil briefly each morning, at which time they discussed the mundane. Sometimes Katie cooked; other times, Neil brought something home. They ate in front of the television set so they didn't have to talk, then Katie took her bath and went to bed and read until she fell asleep.

On Friday she attended her doctor's appointment. Dr. Chambers was a middle-aged man with an easy smile. Katie had been seeing him for years and felt comfortable with him. Once he'd examined her, he met with her briefly in his office. They were just finishing their discussion when his nurse tapped on the door and peeked in. ''Katie, your husband is here. May I bring him back?''

Katie knew her mouth was hanging open. ''My husband?'' she managed. She looked at Dr. Chambers. ''Is it okay?''

''Of course.''

A moment later Neil stepped inside. ''Sorry I'm late,'' he said, pausing to drop a kiss on Katie's head. He introduced himself to Dr. Chambers, and they shook hands.

"So this is the lucky man. Congratulations to you both." He turned to Neil. "Mr. Logan, your wife is approximately fourteen weeks pregnant and doing very well."

"That's good news."

The doctor turned to Katie. "I'll need to see you next month, and schedule you for an ultrasound. I don't expect any problems. You're healthy as a horse."

Neil cleared his throat. "Do you think Katie will have trouble during delivery?" he asked. "I mean with her being built small."

Katie looked at him, surprised by the question.

"I don't think it will present a problem unless the pregnancy progresses well past her due date, but I'll be watching closely and measuring the baby as time goes on." He clasped his hands together on the desk. "See you next month, Katie."

Katie didn't say anything to Neil until they'd left the office. "How did you know I was here?" she asked.

"I saw it on the calendar this morning as I was leaving for work. Sorry I was late."

She stopped in the hall. "Neil, I don't expect—"

"I know, I know. I just wanted to be there for support. Is that okay?"

Katie began walking again. She wasn't sure *how* she felt about him being there in that capacity. "Our agreement was that you would give my baby a name, simple as that."

They exited the building. It was a beautiful fall day, but Neil didn't see it. He felt like an idiot. "I won't go next time."

He turned, but Katie grabbed his sleeve. "Neil, I'm sorry. I didn't mean to sound critical. I just feel so lost right now."

He faced her. "Where are you parked?"

She pointed in the direction of her car.

"Let's sit inside for a moment and talk." They headed

for her car. Once inside, Neil looked at her. "What's on your mind, Katie?"

She was determined to maintain her composure. "I'm just feeling scared right now, okay? I'm three and a half months pregnant, and I don't know the first thing about being a mother." She leaned her forehead against the steering wheel and sighed.

"You're going to be a wonderful mother, Katie, so stop worrying."

"We're both so tense," she said after a moment. "We've been tiptoeing around each other, trying to stay out of each other's way."

He regarded her. "You know damn well *why* things are so tense between us, Katie."

Of course she knew. It had started with the kiss. She remained silent.

Neil opened his door and put one foot on the pavement. "Tell you what. Go home and take a bubble bath, and I'll take you out to dinner. We can see a movie if you like."

"Do you think that's wise?"

He raked his hand through his dark hair. "I don't know anymore. I just want to take you to dinner, okay? Let's not make a big deal out of it." He climbed from the car. "I'll be home around six. Won't take me long to get ready." He smiled slightly. "Don't fog up the house with all that powder."

Katie watched him hurry away. Lord, Lord, what had she done? She had spent the last fifteen minutes telling him how confused she was where their relationship was concerned, only to have Neil invite her out. She was going on a date with Neil Logan, and to make matters worse, she was looking forward to it.

By the time Neil arrived home, Katie was dressed and waiting. He stopped short when he noticed the plum-colored sweaterdress that hugged every curve and showed off her perfect legs. He gave a low whistle. "Lookin' good, Katie Lee."

Bruno hurried over, as though he thought the whistle was for him.

Katie blushed. "I figured I should wear it while I still can," she confessed. She patted her tummy. "Won't be long before I'm in baggy blouses and elastic waistbands."

Neil eyed her stomach as Bruno licked his hand. He wondered how long it would take for her to start showing. "You don't look pregnant," he said, thinking out loud.

"It won't be long."

He gave Bruno a pat on the head. "I'm going to grab a quick shower," he said, deciding the last thing he needed to think about was the baby growing inside her. It brought to mind warm, soft, feminine places that he had no business pondering. He'd wanted to spend the evening with her so they could settle things between them, learn to relax around each other and stop the tiptoeing around, as Katie had put it.

Katie checked her makeup twice and studied her reflection in the full-length mirror as she waited for Neil. Bruno came into the room, a dejected look on his face. "Poor boy," she said, scratching him beneath his chin. "You haven't had a lot of attention lately, have you?" The dog wagged his tail and gazed up at her with loving brown eyes. Katie wondered how animals could love so easily while humans did their best to make a mess of it.

They dined at a local seafood place and then went to the movies to see a love story Katie had chosen.

When they exited the movie theater two hours later, Katie was mopping her eyes with a tissue. Neil helped her inside his Jeep. "There's a box of tissues in my glove compartment if you need more," he said, having sat through the last twenty minutes of the movie listening to her sniffling and growing more irritated by the minute.

"You're angry with me."

"No, confused is a better word. It's not enough that your hormones are hopping all over the place and you cry at the drop of a hat these days. You had to choose a damn tearjerker."

"I didn't know the hero was going to die at the end," she said, blowing her nose. She punched the button on the glove compartment and reached for the small box of tissues inside. "And they were so much in love."

Neil started the engine and backed out of the parking slot. "It was just a movie, Katie. It didn't really happen."

Nevertheless, Katie sniveled all the way home. Neil continued to shake his head and wonder at the complexities of women. "Are you going to be okay?"

"Y-yes. I know you think I'm being silly, but I can't help it." She hiccuped. "I just get so emotional. One minute I'm happy, the next minute I'm ready to burst into tears over nothing."

"It's called pregnancy," he said, reaching over to pat her hand. He let it rest there awhile. "You'll live through it." He wasn't so certain he would.

Genna phoned early the next morning. "I thought I should give you the news," she told Katie. "Drew Hastings is back in town. Word has it he's married."

Neil was reading the newspaper when Katie stormed from her bedroom a few minutes later, looking as though she had murder on her mind. She headed for the kitchen.

"Are we having a mood swing, Katie Lee?"

She swung around, hands on hips. "That was Genna. Drew is back from his extended vacation."

Neil froze. He had known the man would return eventually, but he'd tried to push it from his mind. "How do you feel about it?"

"I'm still mad as hell over what he did to me and your family, but I think I should tell him about the baby. I wonder how his new wife will take the news," she said, sarcasm creeping into her voice.

"Wife?" Neil folded the paper.

"Seems he married his old girlfriend while they were visiting Jamaica, using *our* honeymoon package."

"We've already decided he's a creep, but I agree with you about the baby. He has a right to know. When do you want to tell him?"

"Immediately. I want to get it over with."

"Do you have any idea where to reach him?"

"I would imagine he and his *bride* are living in the house we leased." She reached for her purse. "I have the phone number somewhere." She fumbled through it, found her wallet and searched for the slip of paper on which she'd written the number. She made for the phone and dialed, punching buttons with a vengeance. Drew answered on the second ring.

"Meet me at the Country Kitchen in an hour," she told him. When he tried to object, she insisted. "Be there." Katie hung up and faced Neil, who was already getting up from the sofa.

"I'm going with you," he said.

She opened her mouth to object, then thought better of it. If ever she needed Neil's support, it was now.

They arrived at the Country Kitchen precisely at eleven o'clock. Drew was nowhere in sight. Katie and Neil selected a booth near the door and waited. Neil drank coffee while Katie sipped water. They had put off ordering breakfast until they settled their business.

Ten minutes later a harried Drew Hastings hurried

through the door, spotted them right away and stepped up to the booth. Neil got up and slid in beside Katie.

"Good to see you again, Hastings," Neil said. "Have a seat."

Drew slid into the seat across from Neil, his brow furrowed in confusion. "What's going on?"

The waitress appeared and refilled Neil's cup. She looked at Drew. "Coffee?"

"He won't be staying," Neil said. The woman nodded and walked away.

Drew regarded Katie. "What's *he* doing here?" he said, motioning to Neil. The two men had never liked each other.

Katie studied Drew's face. His nose was too thin, too pointed at the end. His chin was weak, not strong and square like Neil's. And his hair, a bland brown color, was not rich and thick like Neil's. She wondered what she had ever seen in him.

"Katie?" Neil nudged her lightly. He would hold off saying anything for the moment.

She realized the men were waiting. "Neil and I are married," she said. "He's here for support."

Drew looked stunned. "You're married?" He glanced from one to the other. "You're kidding, right? The two of you never even liked each other."

Neil put his arm around Katie. "I've been in love with this woman for years. That's why I tried to talk her out of marrying you. But Katie is a noble woman. She felt it was her duty to marry you, even if it meant living in a dull, lifeless marriage and never experiencing an orgasm."

Katie felt the blood rush to her face. What in heaven's name was Neil doing?

Drew's face turned apple-red as he regarded Neil. "That was highly inappropriate."

"Hey, I'm just trying to help you out, bubba. Sounds like you need it."

Drew looked at Katie, his eyes resentful. It was obvious he suspected she was talking out of turn. "You want the money for the Jamaica trip, right?" He reached into his jacket for a checkbook.

"I'm glad you were able to use both tickets," she said coolly.

He ignored the remark as he filled out the check in his neat handwriting and signed it. From a separate pocket, he pulled out a handful of receipts. "This should cover everything," he said, sliding the check and receipts toward her. "Anything else?"

Katie put them into her purse and clasped her hands on the table, looking him dead in the eye. "I'm four months pregnant."

The color drained from Drew's face. "Is this some kind of joke?" he managed. "Are you trying to get back at me for what I did?"

Neil shifted in his seat but remained silent.

"Don't be ridiculous," she said.

"Me, ridiculous? You're four months pregnant, and this is the first I hear of it?"

"I didn't find out until I was almost three months. I was going to surprise you with it on our honeymoon. You told me you wanted to start a family right away. In fact, that's all you talked about."

He looked away. He simply stared out at the parking lot. Neil and Katie remained silent. Finally Drew turned to Katie. "What are you planning to do about it?"

"I'm going to have the baby."

He sighed and shook his head. "Katie, you need to think. I'm married. You're married. My wife wants to get pregnant right away, biological clock and all that." He smiled as though trying to make a joke, but it fell flat. He cleared his throat. "This news comes at a very bad time."

"It wasn't exactly convenient for Katie, either," Neil

said, "but she's made her decision, and the family is supporting her. I only hope to God the kid doesn't have your nose."

Drew seemed to take offense. "Is that the real reason you married her?" He looked smug. "Because she's pregnant?"

Neil balled his fists in his lap. He wanted to punch the man, and he knew it would only end up embarrassing Katie. "Don't piss me off, Hastings," he said, his tone menacing, "and don't ever, *ever* try to belittle my wife or you'll rue the day. You screwed up royally when you let her go." He looked at Katie, and his voice was gentle when he spoke. "I married her because she's beautiful, sexy, sweet and probably the brightest woman I've ever met. And because I love her and only want the best for her."

Katie saw the look in his eyes, and it almost stole her breath. She was so taken with his words she couldn't think of a response.

Drew seemed to ponder the situation. "How do I know you weren't seeing each other during our engagement? How do I know the baby belongs—"

"Don't do it," Neil said, his voice sounding more dangerous than before. "This is my last warning." He placed his hands on the table, palms down, and leaned forward, putting his face as close to the other man's as he could. "Don't ask the next question or I will drag you out into the parking lot and make you wish you'd never been born. And I'll get away with it, boy, trust me."

Katie froze. She had never seen this side of Neil. He had been well trained in the art of intimidation. It was scary.

Drew seemed to sense he was treading on dangerous ground. He had tested Neil's limits and been unwise in doing so. His demeanor changed immediately. "All I'm suggesting is a simple paternity test," he said politely.

Neil drummed his fingers on the table, never taking

his eyes off the man. He was itching for a fight. "No problem."

Katie placed one hand on Neil's. "That may not be necessary, Drew," she said, trying to keep the situation under control. "The reason I called you here is because I'm asking you to sever all rights to this child."

He looked surprised.

"I only thought it was fair to tell you about the pregnancy," she added. "You certainly have a right to know."

"That's it?" he asked.

She nodded. "I plan to have my attorney draw up the papers immediately."

Drew took a moment to consider it. Neil watched his facial expressions and wondered what was going through the man's head. He was obviously weighing his options. If he maintained contact with his child, he and Katie would have a connection that would give him carte blanche into what Neil's mother called "polite society." It might open a few doors for him professionally. He was also in the position of asking for joint custody and, with a good attorney, could benefit financially if something happened to Katie, who stood to inherit a lot of money one day.

"Before you make your decision, let me say this," Neil began. "My father keeps several of Atlanta's best lawyers on retainer because of the magazine. He will go to all lengths to see that you never get a dime from this family. In fact, my father is expecting money from you. He's suing you for the cost of the wedding and the reception. I've seen the figures. You could buy a couple of BMWs with what you owe."

Drew looked pale.

"Speaking of money," Katie said. "Should you decide to maintain your rights as the biological father, I'll need child support and educational expenses. I intend to see that this child attends the best private schools, and when college time rolls around, I will insist on nothing less than an Ivy League school. My attorney will need to see your financial records from time to time. I trust your accountant will cooperate.'' She paused for air. ''In return, I will be more than generous with visitation once the baby is born. How about every weekend?'' She knew how Drew loved golfing and sailing on weekends.

Drew looked angry enough to eat Neil's coffee cup. ''You've got it all figured out, haven't you?'' he said to Katie. He slid from the booth. ''Have your lawyer send me the paperwork,'' he said. ''I'll sign away all rights immediately.'' He shoved the glass door hard on his way out.

Neil and Katie exchanged looks. ''Well, that's that,'' she said.

''You okay?''

''Yup. Let's order breakfast.'' She tried to sound pleased with the way things had turned out, but it was difficult not to feel a real sense of disappointment where Drew was concerned. She had expected him to fight for his unborn child, to demand his rights as a father. The only reason he had hesitated was because he'd been weighing his options with regard to future gains, and Neil had been savvy enough to pick up on it.

Drew had just rejected her all over again, this time in Neil's presence. It was almost more than she could bear, but she'd be darned if she would let it show.

Eight

Several weeks later Neil arrived home late, only to find Katie wearing a pink leotard and tights, exercising in front of the TV set. He paused just inside the door and stared. She was so caught up in the video that she obviously hadn't heard him come in. She presently had her hands clasped around her ankles, doing some sort of squatting thing, that gave him a clear shot of her behind.

He groaned inwardly. *Katie, Katie, Katie.* He stood there, transfixed, as Bruno lumbered over and licked him on the hand. He stroked the dog's head but never took his eyes off the woman in pink. She reminded him of the ballerina that had danced on her music box, the one he'd given her for Christmas when she was nine years old. His parents had forced him to buy her a gift with his very own money that year. He had found the music box on a sale table at one of the discount stores for less than five bucks. Katie's eyes had widened in delight when she'd opened the gift. She had always wanted one, she'd said, carrying it upstairs and putting it in a prominent place on her dressing table. He'd felt guilty for begrudging her what little money he'd spent on her.

He watched her closely as she finished the exercise and stretched, much as the woman on the video was doing. As Katie reached for the ceiling, the muscles in her body flexed. She squeezed her buttocks, and it was his undoing. He imagined running his hand over each one, feeling the smooth skin beneath his palm. He longed to stroke her inner thighs, to press his lips against them and inhale her scent. And that softly rounded tummy, more pronounced in her present outfit, enticed him. How could he feel such desire toward a pregnant woman?

Neil realized he was aroused.

Katie sensed she wasn't alone. She turned and found Neil standing just inside the door, watching. She blushed, leaned forward and pressed the stop button. "Hi. I was just trying to get my exercises out of the way before dinner."

Neil quickly made his way into the kitchen, standing behind the counter so that his lower body was hidden from sight. He was hard now. "Don't let me stop you," he said.

"I was just finishing up. Stretching out my muscles."

He thought about the muscle behind his zipper. He was aware of a gentle throbbing sensation, an ache that wouldn't go away. To distract himself, he turned for the refrigerator and grabbed a root beer. "How long have you been exercising?" he asked, trying to make simple conversation.

"A couple of weeks. I try to do it before you get home so you can watch the news. Are you hungry?"

"Huh?"

Katie noticed he was acting strangely. "Dinner is in the oven. I hope you're in the mood for baked chicken and vegetables. I'm turning over a whole new leaf, only healthy foods allowed in the house from now on.''

Neil couldn't tell her what he was in the mood for. "Chicken is fine. Do I have time to grab a quick shower?"

"Sure."

Neil waited for her to move, but she didn't. He kept standing there sipping his root beer, wishing she'd go inside her bedroom so he could hurry, unnoticed, toward his own. "If you want to shower first, that's okay," he offered. "I'll set the table."

She hesitated. "Are you sure? You sounded like you really wanted one."

"No, no, I can wait. You go ahead."

She shrugged and started for the kitchen. "I need a drink of water first."

"I'll get it." Neil reached for the overhead cabinet and pulled out a glass. He filled it with water and passed it over the counter.

Katie noticed he was shaking as she took the glass and sipped. He looked tense, the veins in his forehead stood out, and his jaw was tight. Something wasn't right. "Are you ill?" She reached up and felt his cheek to see if he had a fever. He flinched. "Neil, for heaven's sake, what is wrong?"

"Oh, hell," he muttered, shrugging out of his light-weight jacket. "What do you *think* is wrong with me? I walked through the front door and saw you in that outfit, and my body went berserk, okay? I'm hard enough to slam nails through a two-by-four."

Katie blushed profusely. "Oh, my—"

"I'm a human being. A man. Do you think I'm oblivious to you?" He didn't realize he'd raised his voice until he shut up.

"Thank you, Neil." Her own voice was soft.

"For what?" he demanded, both angry and embarrassed.

"I don't feel very attractive right now so I appreciate the compliment."

He just stared. "You don't get it, do you? You could walk around in burlap, and I would get the hots for you."

"I had no idea. Is that why you spend so much time in your room?"

"Yes."

"I'm sorry."

"Sorry?" Neil slung his jacket over the back of a dining chair and regarded her, hands on hips. "You're *sorry?*"

"What do you expect me to say? You're not in this alone, you know. I may be pregnant, but I still have...desires. You're a very handsome and sexy man, Neil. Do you think I'm blind to that?"

He was surprised. "You've never said anything."

"I'm trying to make it easier for both of us."

He closed the distance between them, but he didn't reach for her as he would have liked. "Katie, I'm so damned attracted to you that I sweat bullets every time I think of you sitting naked in your bubble bath. You don't want to know what goes through my mind."

"I think I have an idea." She smiled ruefully. She had entertained thoughts of him in the shower.

"What are we going to do about it?"

She sighed and brushed a lock of hair from her face. "I don't know, Neil. I honestly don't know. The thought of us getting involved...in *that* way...scares me."

It scared the hell out of him, too. But every time he looked into those green eyes he felt as though he were sinking deeper and deeper into something—like quicksand—and he was sinking fast. He had promised to maintain his distance, but that resolve had gone out the window the night he'd kissed her. He was drawn to her, and the bond they'd formed in just a short time baffled him. He didn't exactly know how or when it had happened.

He stepped even closer and encircled her waist with his arms. He noted the cautious look in her eyes. She stiffened at first, then relaxed, but wouldn't meet his gaze. He pulled her closer until she was flush against him. He simply held her. He needed to feel her closeness, absorb the sweetness that was uniquely Katie. She was soft and curvy in all the right places. He traced his fingers along the small of her back, touching each vertebra. Katie shivered and laid her head against his chest. They both sighed pleasantly.

"Do you have any idea what it's been like for me with you living right under the same roof?" he asked, his lips touching her forehead. He could smell her shampoo. It wasn't the fruity scent he'd smelled on other women, it was a clean, soapy smell with only a whisper of something nice.

"Should I move out?" she asked.

"Hell, no. I'd go crazy."

"Is this the same man who valued his privacy above all else?" There was a teasing lilt to her voice.

"You don't crowd me, Katie, you blend into my life perfectly. It's like…well, I can't explain it. I used to enjoy coming home to an empty house, my place of refuge as I saw it. Now I look forward to finding you here."

"I like being here."

"But it's not enough. I want to make love to you, hold you in my arms until you fall asleep. I want to be able to reach out and touch you in the night, I want to open my eyes in the morning and find you next to me." He shook his head. "Why are we fighting this?"

"Perhaps because it's happening too quickly." There were other reasons, of course, but she didn't want to go into them.

"Happening too quickly?" he echoed. "Damn, Katie, we've known each other all of our lives."

That much was true. Having lived under the same roof

so many years, Katie knew Neil better than anyone. His likes and dislikes, the way his hair fell across his forehead when he climbed out of bed each morning. She knew how he sometimes forgot to put the top back on his toothpaste, that when he was running late in the morning, he sometimes tossed his underwear and bath towel into the shower until he could get to it later. She knew he could not sleep in his bed without mussing all the covers, unlike her, who awoke each morning with the other half of her bed as neat as it had been when she went to sleep the night before. His idea of making a bed was pulling the comforter up, leaving his blanket and sheet tangled beneath it.

Neil hooked his finger beneath her chin and raised her head, tilting it back so he was looking directly into her eyes. What was he seeing there? Anxiety? Confusion? He didn't blame her; he felt it, too. But there was more. She had confessed feeling much the same as he did, and the emotions playing across her face gave her a look of vulnerability that tugged at his heart.

He hated seeing her nervous, especially when it concerned him. He wished he could take it all away and fill her with a sense of well-being. As he gazed down at her, her lips parted, and he was no more able to resist her than he was his next breath. Slowly he bent his head and captured her lips. The minute he made contact, he felt that sense of sinking again. Every muscle in his body tensed. His stomach felt odd, as though a flock of geese had just taken flight. Butterflies, he thought. The woman gave him butterflies.

Katie felt Neil's kiss deepen, and all logical thought ceased. His tongue was slow, running against her bottom lip lightly, before tasting the inside of her mouth. He teased her own tongue until she met his and followed it past his lips. His mouth was hot and tasted of him, with only a hint of the gum he chewed when he had something on his mind.

She felt him slide his hands down her back and cover her hips, and she was helpless to stop him. He anchored her tightly against him. She could feel him hard against her.

Oh, Lord. What to do, what to do?

Neil broke the kiss, and they sucked in air. "Katie," he whispered, his voice barely audible. He could not hear it for the blood rushing in his ears. "The things you do to me." He released her and stepped back, afraid to make another move. "What does this mean, baby?"

A thrill ran through Katie at the endearment. Her heart beat frantically. "I don't know. I don't know."

Neil saw his own confusion mirrored in her eyes. "What should we do?" He felt the same vulnerability he'd seen on her face. He, who always had all the answers, was quick on his feet, led men into dangerous situations and had to make split-second decisions in order to get the job done and protect those who depended on him. Yet he had only to take one look at Katie and his brain turned to mush.

Katie swallowed and tried to get her emotions under control. It was hard to think at the moment with him standing so close. He had never looked more handsome and desirable, and she wanted to go on kissing him forever. She wanted to know what it was like to lie naked in his arms, to feel him inside her. "Perhaps there's a reasonable explanation," she managed, her voice quaking.

"Tell me. I'll listen to anything at this point."

She shook her head, trying to clear it. "Sometimes people meet at a time in their lives when…when it's right."

"We didn't just meet. I've known you for more than twenty years."

"Not like this," she said. "Maybe the timing wasn't right before. I don't know, Neil, honestly I don't. I'm just guessing here."

It was too much for him to take in. She'd been in his home less than two months, and he was fast losing his head over her. She had inched her way into his private life, and had slowly begun chiseling away the barriers he'd built around himself. It scared the hell out of him.

Katie saw the play of emotions on his face. "Let's take it slow, Neil. There are too many issues at hand." His job; her pregnancy. "I need a little time to think."

Neil rounded the cabinet and stood on the other side. He had to put some distance between them or he would pull her back into his arms, and heaven only knew what would happen. They stood there, staring at each other as if for the first time. When the doorbell rang, neither of them moved to answer it for fear of letting go of the moment. It rang again.

Katie blinked. "Aren't you going to answer it?"

Neil sighed and made for the door. He found his neighbor, Naomi Klumpet, on the other side. "Oh, Mrs. Klumpet." He opened the door wide. "Won't you come in?"

The woman stepped inside, caught one look at Katie in her pink exercise wear and smiled. "Oh, my, I didn't know you were expecting," she said, her eyes landing on Katie's stomach.

Neil noted the blush on Katie's cheek. "Yes. We're very excited about it."

"Congratulations! You're a sight to behold, Katie," Naomi continued. "Why, you're literally glowing."

Katie stepped closer. "Thank you, Mrs. Klumpet."

"Please call me Naomi. I'm so sorry I haven't been able to do something nice for the two of you, but my sister has been under the weather for weeks, and I insisted she come stay with me until she's well."

"Oh, but you already have done something nice," Katie said. "The flowers were beautiful."

"So was your thank-you card, dear. Most young people don't bother with things like that anymore." She paused and reached into a pocket on her apron. "The mailman accidentally put a piece of your mail in my mailbox. It's addressed to you, Katie.'' She handed Katie the envelope.

"Thank you, Naomi.'' Katie recognized her attorney's return address and knew it had to do with Drew. "Won't you join us for a glass of iced tea?''

"I can't. Perhaps another time.'' She looked at Neil. "I hope you're taking good care of this little lady. You're going to have to give up your selfish bachelor ways and see to her needs.'' She reached up to pinch his cheek, but he darted out of the way.

"I'll walk you home,'' Neil said, maintaining a safe distance.

"I'm perfectly capable of seeing myself home, young man.''

He knew it was useless to argue with her and watched the woman cross the lawn before he closed the door. "What have you got there?'' he asked Katie.

Katie opened the envelope and pulled out a two-page legal document. "Well now, my lawyer acted quickly on this one, and Drew didn't waste any time signing it.''

"He agreed to give up his rights to the baby?''

"Yep.'' Katie folded the document and replaced it inside the envelope. "That's that.''

Neil could not read the expression on her face. "You okay?''

Katie forced a smile she didn't feel. "Of course I'm okay. I'm the one who requested it, if you'll remember. Now, if you don't mind, I'd like to go ahead and take my bath. You've dawdled so long you've missed your chance to shower first.''

Neil's eyes caressed her. "I wouldn't exactly call it dawdling.''

"The consequences are still the same.'' Katie turned and headed for the bathroom.

An hour later Neil was still waiting for her to come out.

He felt all wrung out, exhausted from the gamut of emotions he'd felt when Katie was in his arms. He was worried about her. She'd been in the bathroom too long. He longed to bang on the door again, find out what was going on, but he thought it best to step back, give her time to herself. She obviously needed it or she wouldn't be in there.

What was she feeling? Was she having second thoughts about dismissing Drew from her life and that of their baby's? Neil couldn't remember when he'd last worried about someone else's feelings other than his own, and it suddenly struck him that he had become self-centered over the years. Just like Mrs. Klumpet had accused him of. Or maybe he always had been.

That didn't mean he didn't care about people or what happened to them; he wouldn't be in his line of work if he didn't. But his job was to serve and protect, and he did it well. If he were sent out on a homicide, he did his level best to solve it, find the murderer and put him behind bars. He was making a difference in the world. Yet he could be selfish at times. He expected someone else to assist the grieving widow or explain to the deceased's children and friends what had happened. He didn't bother trying to answer questions as to why bad things happened and seemingly for no reason. His job was to solve the crime and leave the rest up to someone who was better at dealing with loved ones because...

Neil frowned as he stared up at the ceiling. Because why? He knew the reasons. He didn't want to have to feel their pain or loss. He didn't want to have to remember what it felt like to lose someone so close that it swallowed you up and you came close to losing yourself, as well. He didn't want to have to live with more guilt.

Like with Ryan.

And now Jim Henderson.

* * *

Katie felt a tiny movement inside her belly as she slipped into a fresh satin gown. Usually she became excited, but the only emotion she was experiencing at the moment was disappointment. It showed in her eyes as she combed her wet hair and fluffed it into place. It had been so easy for Drew to walk out of their baby's life, to just sign it over, toss it aside like yesterday's garbage. How could he not look forward to seeing his own son or daughter? It hurt. Not because she fancied reconciliation, but because he had been only too happy to turn his back on what he saw as a problem. An inconvenience, he'd said.

Katie realized how her mother must have felt when the same thing had happened to her. Had her own father ever thought about the child he'd helped create? Had he not wondered if she had been a boy or a girl, or if she had his eyes or nose? Had he not cared that she would be branded illegitimate the rest of her life?

Obviously not. He had never once tried to contact her, if only to see how she'd turned out. No calls, not even an occasional birthday card. He would never know the shame she had felt, how often she'd stood by the fence surrounding the playground, waiting for him to pull up in a shiny new car and reveal himself. In her fantasies, he was always handsome and well-dressed. "You're as beautiful as your mother," he would say. Then he'd whisk her away, and Katie would see the jealous looks of the girls who had taunted her for so long. Her mother would rush into his arms the moment he pulled into their yard, and Katie would stand right beside them in a new pink dress as they said their wedding vows and lived happily ever after.

But that had never happened. She would return to school the following day, a skinny girl who picked wildflowers and sprinkled baby powder on her pillow because it somehow softened the hurt she felt inside.

In her bedroom she walked to the dresser where she'd

left the legal documents, and she very carefully signed her name, sealing her child's fate forever. She put them in an envelope, addressed it to her attorney and put a stamp on it before stuffing it inside her purse.

The house was quiet, as if the people inside were in mourning. Neil's bedroom door was closed. He hadn't eaten anything. Katie put the food in plastic containers, washed and dried the pans and put them away. She set up the coffeepot so when Neil awoke in the morning it would be waiting for him.

She simply stood there, wishing Neil would open the door and come out. If ever there was a time she needed him, it was now. She longed to feel his arms around her again, his lips on hers. She wanted to lie against him, rest her head on his chest, feel his warmth, absorb his strength. But every time he tried to get close, she pushed him away.

Perhaps she, like her mother, would spend the rest of her life alone. She would draw happiness from her child, attending dance recitals or Little League games, become a room mother at school and volunteer to help with parties and school outings. She would be the mom who always had snacks in the cupboards, so when school friends dropped by they would feel welcome. She would immerse herself in her child's life so there would be no time to deal with her own emptiness.

Who was she trying to fool? Katie told herself. She wanted more than that, and she didn't want to end up clinging to her son or daughter simply because she had no one else. She wanted to fall in love, to wake in the night and find the man of her dreams beside her. She wanted someone to snuggle with on cold days, or sleep late and lie in bed sharing the Sunday paper.

She wanted Neil Logan, wanted him more than she'd ever wanted anything in her life.

Katie's hands trembled as she turned his doorknob.

Neil's room was dark as she entered. He must have showered at some point, because she caught the scent of soap and clean male flesh. She heard him shift on the bed.

"Katie?" he called out softly.

She wasn't surprised he'd awakened so easily. Neil was a cop, his senses sharper than the average person's. "Neil?"

He reached for the lamp and switched it on. Katie stood there like an angel in white satin, her face scrubbed, blond hair whispering against her shoulders. He could smell her from where he lay, the powdery scent he had come to expect when he walked through the front door. She looked anxious, uncertain. "What is it, babe?" he asked.

Katie gazed at him. He wore navy boxers, cut high on dark, hair-roughened thighs. His chest looked massive, that same dark hair glistening beneath the lamplight. He had never looked more appealing, dark and sexy, a stray curl falling over his forehead. Even reclining on the bed, he looked strong and powerful.

The look in his eyes questioned her. She stepped closer to the bed, reached for the hem of her gown and pulled it over her head. She let it go, and it floated to the floor silently. She noted the expression on Neil's face, outright astonishment, but also a look of desire so intense that she knew he found her beautiful despite her pregnancy.

"I don't want to sleep alone tonight," she said.

Nine

Neil bolted upright on his bed, his thoughts reeling at the sight of Katie's nakedness. Every nerve in his body sprang to life at the sight of her, more beautiful than anything he'd ever imagined. He climbed from the bed and approached her slowly, half-afraid he was dreaming and that if he moved too quickly she would disappear. His eyes met hers and locked. He saw the need and longing in her green eyes, that same need that had become so much a part of his own life the time she'd been there. He longed to reach out, encircle her waist, pull her flush against him so he could feel her sweet body.

"Are you sure, Katie?" he whispered.

"Yes."

Without taking his eyes off her face, he scooped her high in his arms and carried her the short distance to the bed. Still holding her, he sat on the bed and pressed his lips to her hair, her forehead, her cheek. He kissed her closed eyes, paused and looked at her. How could a woman appear so angelic and sexy at the same time? he wondered. And how could a man want to pay homage to her one moment and lose himself in her the next?

He kissed her lips gently, parting them with his tongue with measured slowness, so it would not seem invasive to her. The sweetness inside was intoxicating. Her tongue greeted him, and he took it into his own mouth. He slid his hand into her hair, letting the silky strands slide through his fingers like spun gold. Everything about her was soft and sweet-smelling and very feminine. She reminded him of everything that was good: sunshine and freshly mown grass, bread baking in the oven and families laughing and fanning themselves on a summer day as they sipped iced tea on a wide front porch.

Then there was the Katie he desired above all else: her lush breasts, the swell of her belly and her smooth thighs drove his thoughts in another direction. His kiss deepened. Hungrily, he tasted the inside of her mouth, wondering if he would ever get enough. He took her bottom lip in his mouth and sucked gently. Katie slipped her arms around his neck and pulled him closer.

After a time Katie's lips felt numb. She no longer knew where hers left off and Neil's began. She suspected he was trying to go slow, give her time to adjust to him, but her body was aching for more. Finally he stood, turned and placed her gently on the bed. He stripped off his boxers, and Katie could only gaze in fascination and feminine appreciation at his maleness. He lay down beside her and gathered her into his arms. She felt him full and hard against her thighs, and her pulse quickened, sending frantic messages to the rest of her body. Her belly warmed, and the heat spread downward, creating an ache so deep she had trouble catching her breath. Neil explored her breasts, taking great care in case they were tender. He slid his palm over her round belly, and her cheeks turned pink.

"Katie." His voice was a hush, a mere whisper, but there was a huskiness to it. "Don't ever be ashamed of how you look right now, because I have never seen a sexier woman." It was true. She had traded, at least temporarily, her snug designer suits in black, navy, gray and red for a softer look. Pastel colors that flowed over her full breasts and hung loosely just above her knees. Pink and yellow and mint-green sweatsuits, accompanied by a matching bow in her hair that made her look like a young girl. And now, wearing absolutely nothing, with the added weight in her hips and thighs, she had ripened into a woman in every sense of the word.

Neil felt more masculine beside her, more virile.

Instincts, as old as time, made him want to protect her and the baby in her womb.

He lowered his head and tongued her nipples until they quivered and tightened. Katie's stomach did a little flipflop as he continued to work his magic. He slipped a knee between her thighs and pressed, and it was her undoing, making her anxious for more. She arched against his thigh.

"Neil!" She cried his name against his neck as the first thrilling sensation shot through her.

Neil tried to maintain control, but it was impossible where Katie was concerned. He kissed the valley between her breasts and ran his lips across her abdomen. Take your time, Logan, he cautioned. Finally, he slipped between her thighs and tasted her for the first time.

For Katie time stood still.

She whimpered at the intimate contact. For a moment it felt as though her heart had stopped beating. Neil's tongue was wet and soft and so gentle, like a butterfly's wing. His warm breath fanned her thighs. She waited, every nerve ending crying out for more. He dipped his head again and found the little bud that ached for his next touch. He teased her, pulled back and waited until she pleaded for more. Only then did he allow himself to apply more pressure, encircling her with the very tip of his tongue as she pressed against him and anchored her fingers in his hair.

Her climax was powerful, and a thing of beauty for Neil to experience. Katie rode his mouth as wave after wave crashed through her, subsiding only seconds before the next. The intensity of it rocked her, shattering all coherent thought and sending her over the edge, as Neil's name became a reverent chant. Neil waited until she grew still before raising his head and gazing into the softest eyes he'd ever seen.

Unable to resist a second more, he swept her legs open and entered her, slowly at first, following the heat. The muscles inside her body gripped him tightly, and he closed his eyes, because the feel of her was as humbling as it was powerful. He paced himself, waiting for her body to respond. Once again she rose to meet him, and they moved in perfect unison. Neil gritted his teeth when Katie closed her legs around his waist, abandoning herself.

He could no longer hold on. The pleasure was too much. Liquid pulsed through his body, white-hot desire that hit him in waves and stole all thought except for the woman beneath him. He felt himself drain into her body, and he shuddered as he felt the last wave come crashing down around him.

Katie lay there waiting for their breathing to become normal again. A single tear slipped down her cheek, and she tried to bring her emotions under control and put a name to what had just happened between them.

Exquisite. It was the only word that came to mind.

Neil paused the moment he saw the tear. "Are you okay?" he whispered.

She smiled, even as the tear made a lazy trail to her jaw. "I am now."

Neil shook his head as what felt like an aftershock rolled through him. He pulled himself up and lay by her, drawing her into his arms. She snuggled against him, shivering like a kitten that had just come in from the rain. Neil reached for the comforter and pulled it over them.

They drifted. Finally Katie climbed from the bed and walked into his bathroom. Neil's eyes followed, studying her as one would a work of art. She returned a few minutes later, and he opened his arms to receive her.

"Katie, I wish I could tell you—"

She put a finger to his lips. She did not want Neil to say anything that might make him feel obligated to her in the future. "Please don't say anything, Neil. Let's just enjoy the moment."

Neil had been about to tell her how wonderful making love with her had been, how it had stirred him so deeply, to his very soul. Why was she trying to prevent him from saying what he felt when he ached so desperately to tell her? Did she not want to hear the truth? That he suspected he was falling in love with her? His brow puckered as he ran through a mental list of what it was that Katie did not want to hear from him.

He knew the moment she fell asleep, her soft steady breathing telling him she'd drifted off. He turned on his side and slipped his arm around her waist. The feel of her naked body against his was something he'd only begun to dream of lately when he had trouble falling asleep. And he'd had his share of sleepless nights since Katie had arrived.

He lay awake for a long time, enjoying the feel of her in his arms, the gentle rise and fall of her chest, the smell of her hair. He thought about the baby growing inside her. He knew nothing about pregnancy, except what he'd experienced with Katie, and he suspected she kept a lot to herself. Now he wanted to know everything.

Katie awoke in the night and reached for Neil. He was there, warm and inviting. He kissed her deeply, his hand delving between her thighs, fingers teasing her to wetness. He entered her, and in the dark they made love slowly, their minds sluggish from sleep. Once again they were lifted to another place, and their soft moans rode the night breeze coming through the window. Satiated, they collapsed in each other arms and slept.

Neil was waiting for Katie when she arrived home. She'd left him sleeping that morning, hoping the quiet time getting dressed would give her a chance to think about how they'd spent the previous night. She had thought of little else all day. Now Neil scooped her high in his arms and carried her toward his bedroom, pulling her low heels off as he went. Their gazes locked, revealing both their anticipation and longing. They smiled and fell onto the bed laughing, but the moment turned serious as soon as their lips met. They kissed deeply, leisurely, as if they had all the time in the world—slow and intoxicating. Lips parted. Tongues mingled. Tasting, tasting, until the heat began to build.

Slowly Neil undressed her, kissing each spot he bared as Katie shivered in delight. Her bra was lacy, and her breasts, peeking over the material like half moons, enticed him. And those damn panties that showed more than they hid. "These things should be outlawed," he said, his voice suddenly husky. He slid his finger along the lacy edges of her crotch, where golden curls peeked out seductively and made him crazy. Her thigh-highs were his undoing, exposing the soft white flesh between their lacy bands and her panties. He stroked her thighs. Had anything ever felt so silky? he wondered. He grew hard.

Katie unbuttoned his shirt with fingers made clumsy by impatience. "Let a professional do this," he said, shrugging out of his clothes in seconds and rejoining her on the bed.

"Show-off." Katie offered him her back, pretending to pout.

Neil smacked her fanny playfully and raised her hair off her neck, kissing her nape until the downy hair stood on end and her skin prickled. He nudged her bottom with his hardness and her breath quickened. Finally he reached between her thighs and teased her until she was wet.

"Oh, Neil!"

"What, baby?"

She opened her thighs wider, and he slipped his finger inside, pulling it out now and then so he could tease the small bud once again. She gasped and held his hand in place. He chuckled and pressed himself against her soft bottom. He had suspected beneath that proper exterior waited a woman of passion, and his suspicions had been correct. He continued to kiss her neck and nibble her earlobes until she drew her thighs tight around his hand and trembled.

When Katie faced him, she tossed him a naughty smile and straddled him, guiding him inside her warmth. Neil rolled his eyes. "I'm a dead man."

She moved against him, slowly at first, waiting for his passion to build. She watched his face, wanting to remember always the passion that made him so strikingly handsome. He moved inside her—slowly, deliberately, his eyes darker with desire. He stroked her breasts, pinching her nipples ever so lightly, a satisfied look on his face when they tightened.

Katie rode him carefully, cautiously, shivering each time she felt him reach higher, embedding himself deeply inside her. He stroked her belly, brushed the curls between her thighs, until he found what he was looking for. Katie threw back her head and moved against him faster. Her body vibrated, every nerve seemed to come alive, sharpening all her senses. The heaviness in her breasts, the warmth of Neil's palms when he cupped them. The ache, low in her belly, moving downward, coiling tight. Tighter and tighter still. The musky scent of male and female, filling the air like an intoxicant. The rhythm of mating, Neil thrusting, bringing her closer. The edge now within reach. Katie paused at the precipice for one heartbeat before tumbling.

She arched against him. Neil cupped her hips with his hands, filling her, pulling away, filling her again. He gritted his teeth tightly as he tried to hold on to the last sane thought in his head. Their movements became frenzied— man and woman racing to the finish until they both cried out as each discovered the pain of so much pleasure.

As soon as he was able to think rationally, Neil cupped Katie's face between his palms and raised it for a kiss. He noticed her moist eyes. "Oh, God, I did hurt you, didn't I?" he said, knowing it must have something to do with her pregnancy.

She shook her head and offered him a tremulous smile. "No, Neil. You brought me back to life."

That night she moved into his bedroom. Neil ordered pizza, and they ate it in bed while they watched TV. When he turned off the light, Katie was beside him, head tucked in the crook of his arm. She felt safe, protected, cherished.

Katie was well into her fifth month of pregnancy when Halloween arrived. She dressed in a pumpkin suit stuffed with newspaper and her protruding abdomen. She wore black tights and orange sneakers on her feet. Neil took one look at her and burst into laughter.

"Don't laugh," she said. "I rented one for you, as well.

You're going to be Mr. Pumpkin and hand out chocolate bars to the trick-or-treaters.''

"Oh, no I'm not."

She smiled sweetly. "Oh, yes you are."

"Hell no. I'm not. What if someone from the force sees me? What if Mrs. Klumpet comes by?"

Katie stepped closer and pulled his shirttail from his jeans. "Don't even try," he said. "You can use all the feminine wiles you want, but I'm not wearing a pumpkin suit."

Katie unfastened the button of his jeans and worked the zipper down. Neil stood there stoically, but he could feel the beads of sweat popping out on his forehead. "Oh, Neil," she said on a sigh. She pressed her breasts against him. As Katie slipped her hand inside his jeans and gripped him with her fingers, Neil mentally cursed the power she had over him. He was as hard as a fence post.

"We still have about half an hour before the goblins come out," she whispered, nipping his chin lightly with her teeth.

Neil groaned.

An hour later Neil was wearing the pumpkin outfit and passing out candy to trick-or-treaters. As he'd feared, Dave and Marjorie showed up with their crew. Dave took one look at Neil, opened his mouth to say something, then closed it at the look Neil shot him.

"Neil, why don't you get our guests a drink?" Katie suggested, as she doled out candy to the children. She barely had time to close the door before the bell rang again. "And pull out the chips and dip while you're at it."

Neil saw that Dave was trying his best to keep a straight face. He took Marjorie a diet soft drink before going back into the kitchen to grab Dave a cold beer. The other man followed, pretending to study the crown molding near the ceiling. "Go ahead and get it out of your system," Neil said. "You're about to bust a gut."

Dave, in the process of drinking his beer, almost choked as he burst into laughter. He wiped his mouth on his sleeve. "I believe she has your number, Logan." He tossed his empty beer can into the trash and slapped Neil on the back. "See you next Halloween, buddy. I'll try to remember to bring along some of the guys."

Katie celebrated her sixth month at Thanksgiving. She had never felt better. She arrived at work one morning and announced they would be remodeling the store. Genna and Doris looked at her as though she'd lost her mind. "I want to clear the large storage room upstairs, move everything to the attic, so we can use the storage area as a children's section."

"Why are you doing this *now?*" Genna had asked. "You shouldn't be lugging books around."

"I've been wanting a children's book section for months. And I've hired a couple of teenage boys to help."

They worked on the project for two weeks. The carpenters had agreed to put in a few hours at night when the store closed for business, and the painters were scheduled to work the second weekend of December, coming in after the store closed on Saturday. As a precaution, Katie planned to take several days off after the painting was completed, not only to avoid any possible fumes, but so she could write out her Christmas cards and shop.

She and Neil bought a tree, something he'd never bothered to do. Since he had no decorations, they headed for the local Wal-Mart and filled the shopping cart with ornaments and a tree stand. They spent two evenings Christmas shopping, and Katie was thankful to have it out of the way.

When Katie returned to work, she was delighted to find everything finished. A friend of Genna's had painted a mural on one wall, the carpenters had built shelves that the children could easily reach and the child-size furniture Katie had ordered from a specialty catalog had arrived. They'd already advertised and sent out flyers announcing the changes and a children's hour to be held every Wednesday around lunchtime. During that time Katie or Genna would read from a new book while the kids ate peanut butter and jelly sandwiches and drank milk from a carton, in order to prevent spills. As Katie had hoped, the children's mothers joined friends in the little eating area. The crowd grew, forcing Katie to move the tables closer together in the dining area and add more.

Katie was so excited about the new project she convinced Neil to come by and take a look.

"The place looks great," he said, over a turkey, bacon and brie sandwich spread with strawberry jam. He teased Katie about serving sissified food. "It should boost business."

"That's what we're hoping for."

He closed his hands over hers. "I'm glad everything is going well for you, Katie. Your business is booming, and you and the baby are healthy. What more could you ask for?"

She met his gaze. She knew what she wanted, but it came at a high price. She and Neil might be happier than they'd ever been, but she never forgot her fear. She was simply putting it on hold.

"Katie, honey, we need to talk," Neil said, once they'd finished lunch.

The seriousness of his tone made her look up. "What is it?"

He hesitated. "The other reason I stopped by today is that I've been asked to work a stakeout. I don't know exactly how long I'll be gone, a few days, a week maybe, but I'll call when I can."

Katie's heart sank at the thought of Neil being away. And on a stakeout of all things! "Is that why you stopped shaving a couple of days ago?" She'd suspected it had something to do with a case but hadn't asked.

He smiled. "I have to blend."

She looked down at her plate. "Is it dangerous?"

"No."

He was lying and she knew it.

"If you need me for something, call Marjorie. She'll know what to do."

"It's less than two weeks until Christmas, Neil." She knew she was whining and hated herself for it.

"I'll be back in plenty of time, baby." They gazed at each other. "The sooner I'm gone, the sooner I'll return."

"It's going to be lonely."

"For me, too." He smiled. "At least you have Bruno."

She glanced away, not wanting him to see how upset she was.

"I have to go," he said, his tone resigned. "Please take care of yourself. Remember to take your prenatal vitamins, and keep that rubber mat in the bathtub so you don't slip. And don't eat too much chocolate. It has caffeine in it."

"Okay."

"If something happens, if you should go into labor while I'm gone, which you won't," he added, "all the telephone numbers are right beside the phone."

"I know that, Neil. I put them there."

"Oh, and be sure to use the dead bolt on the front door and that metal rod inside the sliding glass doors. I don't want to have to worry about someone breaking in while I'm gone."

"I promise." She finally looked at him, offering the closest thing she had to a smile. "When you get home I'll make your favorite meal."

"As long as I can have you for dessert." His eyes softened. "I'll see you soon." Neil stood and kissed Katie on the top of her head, taking a moment to enjoy her scent. He walked away without another word, but when he climbed into his Jeep a moment later, he patted his pockets, feeling as though he'd left something important behind.

"Katie," he said softly.

Katie had not heard from Neil during the three days he'd been gone. Not one word. He, Dave and another detective were on the stakeout—that much came from Marjorie. "All I know is that it involves a major drug dealer, who the APD suspects committed a number of homicides over the past few years. Neil volunteered for this job. It's important to him."

Katie's mind started working. "Why is it so important? Does it have anything to do with his partner getting shot?"

"I don't know."

Katie sensed Marjorie did know but wasn't saying.

"Try not to worry, honey. Dave hasn't called me, either, but that's not surprising under the circumstances. The department has put three of their top men on the case. These guys know what they're doing."

Katie thought of Jim, who was still recovering from his gunshot wounds.

"I'll be okay," Katie said. They talked for a while. Marjorie asked how she was feeling, how her last doctor's appointment had gone, and suggested they meet for lunch soon. Katie got the impression the woman was trying to take Katie's mind off her worries.

"Just remember this, Katie. It's hard in the beginning, but you get used to it after a while."

Katie knew she would never get used to it. She was still worried when she climbed into Neil's bed. *Why* was the case so important to Neil? Katie wondered. Here she was, in the last trimester of her pregnancy, and he had volunteered for a job that could take days or weeks.

It had to do with Jim Henderson, she thought. Neil would never have left her at this late date unless it was personal. But *why* was Neil taking it so personally, when he had made it clear that she was his top priority now?

Katie almost gasped out loud when the answer came, a flashback from the night in Marjorie's kitchen. A giant fist closed over her heart and squeezed until she thought she would become ill. She covered her face with her hands to keep from crying out.

Neil suspects the bullet was meant for him.

Katie climbed from the bed the following morning feeling exhausted, her anxiety level near the panic stage. She had suffered a fitful night, chock-full of bad dreams. She had dreamed about the day June Logan had told her of her mother's death, the feeling of loss so deep she was unable to cry. She remembered the little black dress June had purchased for her, the hush that had fallen over the house, especially when Katie walked into the room. She saw June and Richard whispering into the phone, searching frantically for Katie's next of kin.

She'd dreamed of Neil. In her dream he was unshaven and wore a purple shirt. Neil never wore purple. She had once read that when you dreamed of someone dressed in purple it meant they were in serious danger.

Katie let Bruno out. The dog seemed to sense a problem because he followed her everywhere. When she accidentally stepped on his paw, he yelped, and she screamed. She sat on the edge of the bed and petted him until they both calmed down.

She put on very little makeup, grabbed her least favorite maternity dress and a pair of sneakers, then left the house without breakfast.

Genna's look was deadpan. "Gee, what have you done with yourself?"

"Not a damn thing," Katie replied. "I'm having a bad day, okay? Can't I have a bad day once in a while? You have bad days, and I don't say anything."

"It's not even eight o'clock. Maybe you're just having a bad morning."

"I plan to stretch it out as long as possible, Genna, so deal with it." She went to her office and slammed the door. Her head throbbed, and her heart felt trapped in the back of her throat. She couldn't just sit there or she'd go crazy. She left her office and went to work.

The day dragged for Katie, and her mood worsened. By three o'clock Genna declared her unfit to deal with customers and sent her to the back office to work on the books. Katie curled up on the sofa and fell asleep. She slept deeply, and her dreams were as unsettling as the night before. When she awoke to someone knocking on her door, she sat up, afraid something terrible had happened. Genna peeked in. "Calm down, it's just me. I brought us hot chocolate with lots of whipped cream."

After apologizing to Genna for behaving like a shrew, Katie headed home, where she found Bruno sprawled on the living-room floor. He didn't raise his head at the sight of her or wag his tail as usual. Katie knelt beside him. "You miss him, too, don't you, boy?"

Bruno just looked at her.

Katie got up and walked into Neil's bedroom. It smelled of him. She stood there for a moment, just looking at it. His bed was made; the room was neat and orderly. And empty. She felt a wave of loneliness that almost took her breath away. She missed him, ached for him in such a way it felt as though even her skin hurt.

Katie dressed in her pink leotard and tights and made a halfhearted attempt to do her exercises. Finally she gave up. She cooked two burgers and gave one to Bruno, who thumped his tail in response. She cleaned up the kitchen, wondering how she would fill the evening. Nothing sounded particularly appealing. She would take a bath and call it a night.

The telephone rang, and she turned around. Probably Genna checking on her to see if she was okay. Poor Genna. Katie answered on the second ring.

"Katie, this is Archer Burns," the voice said from the other end. "I'm sorry to call with bad news, but Neil has been hurt. He's been taken to the emergency room at Mercy. I don't think they're going to be able to help him—"

Fear shot through her, and Katie dropped the phone as if it were a hot iron. Her mind reeled. Neil was in the emergency room, and they couldn't help him. She felt dizzy. Her thoughts raced in one direction, then another. It had to be bad. But hadn't she known all along that something like this would happen?

Katie stumbled toward her purse, praying her knees would not give out. She grabbed her keys from the dining table and raced out the door.

Ten

Katie drove to the hospital in record time, parking as close to the emergency entrance at Mercy as she could. She hurried inside to the reception desk.

"My husband is here," Katie managed to say, gasping for air.

The teenager at the desk did a double take. "Are you a ballerina?"

Katie had forgotten how she was dressed. "The last name is Logan. *L-O-G-A-N*. Where can I find him?"

The girl shrugged. "I'm just covering for the receptionist, who went to the canteen."

"When will she be back?"

"Five minutes, maybe."

"I don't have that long. Open those doors." She pointed to a set of double doors where a sign read No Admittance.

"I don't think I'm supposed to do that."

Katie leaned over the counter so that her face was less

than an inch from the other girl's. "Do it." The girl's eyes widened as she hit a button.

The door buzzed, and Katie pushed through. She started down the hall and bumped into a nurse coming out of an examination room, where a child was shrieking loud enough to shatter glass. Katie grabbed the nurse's arm. "I'm looking for my husband. Neil Logan."

The woman appeared harried, as if she were ready to start pulling out her hair, strand by strand. "Mr. Logan is in room three, but the doctor is still with him." The child wailed, and the nurse winced and turned for the room. "Mrs. Brown, you've simply got to calm your son. He's disturbing everyone on the unit."

"How is he?" Katie said.

The nurse glanced over her shoulder. "We've given him something for pain, but there's really nothing more we can do."

"What do you mean there's nothing more that you can do?" Katie shouted, trying to make herself heard over the screaming child.

"Ma'am, you'll have to talk to his doctor."

Nothing more they can do. That meant there was no hope. Katie stumbled blindly toward the room. She tried to compose herself before going in.

Neil lay flat on his back, eyes closed. Her heart sank. Was he already gone? Perhaps he was in a coma and there was a sliver of hope. She stepped closer. Already he wore a full beard. She looked about. She had expected him to be all bloody, but there was not a drop in sight. A doctor stood nearby, writing something on a clipboard. He looked up. "I'm Dr. Winn. May I help you?"

"I'm Mrs. Logan," she said, her voice trembling badly. "How is he?"

"Well, he's no longer in pain, but it's really out of our hands."

Katie struggled with the words. "Out of your hands?"

Neil opened his eyes. "Katie, is that you?" He sounded groggy.

She rushed to the head of the bed. "Yes, Neil, it's me. I'm here, honey." She grabbed his hand and squeezed it tightly. "Don't let go, Neil. Hang on, sweetie. I promise to stay with you until—" She couldn't very well say until the very end because he might not realize how seriously injured he was. "I'll stay as long as you need me."

He gazed into her eyes. "Did you miss me, baby?"

At least he could see her. She wanted him to see the love on her face as he drew his last breath. "Oh, honey, I missed you so much I couldn't eat or sleep." Her throat was clogged with emotion, and it was all she could do to keep from bursting into tears. Be brave, she told herself. Be brave for Neil.

He offered her a lopsided smile. "We broke the case, baby. We played him like a tune." He closed his eyes for a moment. "He's behind bars tonight."

Katie's eyes filled with tears. "I'm so proud of you," she said. "So very proud." She touched his cheek. "Neil, you have made this world a better place for people like me and the baby. You're a hero. You'll always be my hero."

The doctor cleared his throat and smiled kindly. "Mrs. Logan, perhaps we should let your husband rest."

"I can't leave until I tell him something, Doctor." She had to tell Neil how she felt about him. She had to confess her love, once and for all, so that he could enter the afterlife knowing he'd been adored in this one. "Neil, I—"

"Why don't you tell him on the way home?"

Katie looked at him. "On the way home?" Her stomach did a nosedive. Oh, Lord, the doctor was sending him home to die. How would she manage? She couldn't do it.

"Yes. Like I said, we've done all that we can do here,

other than give him painkillers and muscle relaxants, but I have referred your husband to a good chiropractor—''

She blinked rapidly. "Chiropractor?"

"For his back injury."

"He has a back injury?"

The doctor gave her a funny look. "Mrs. Logan, are you okay?"

"My husband isn't dying?"

Dr. Winn looked startled. "Who on earth told you that?"

"Well, I...I—"

"Your husband wrenched his back jumping over a fence."

Neil opened his eyes and lifted his head slightly. "I was running from a Doberman pinscher, babe. Tried to leap a six-foot fence. I could have done it back in high school."

"You mean he's going to *live?*" Katie insisted.

"Not forever. But he's in good shape, so he's got plenty of years ahead of him."

Katie almost slumped to the floor in relief. The doctor caught her before she fell. "Sit down, Mrs. Logan, you don't look well."

Neil raised himself up, wincing in pain as he did so. "Katie, are you okay?"

"Mr. Logan, you shouldn't be sitting up," the doctor warned.

Katie took a moment to catch her breath. When she did, she shot Neil a dark look. "Why did you let me think you were dying?"

"Dying? Where did you get a crazy idea like that?" He slurred his words badly.

Katie leaped to her feet and closed the distance between them. Here she was, planning Neil's funeral arrangements, and all he'd done was hurt his back. "You *allowed* me to believe you had been fatally injured." She turned to the doctor. "And you! Telling me there was nothing more you could do for my husband."

"We can't. That's why I'm sending him to someone who can."

Katie wasn't listening. "Do you have any idea what I've been through the last half hour?" she shouted so loudly Neil winced. "Do you? I almost totaled my car getting here." She shoved hard against his chest.

Dr. Winn took a step back as though he feared for his own safety. "Mrs. Logan, why don't you wait for your husband in the lobby?"

Neil chanced a look at her. She was mad all right. "Katie, honey, do you realize that if I'd fallen the wrong way, I could have injured my spine and been paralyzed for the rest of my life?"

"That's not good enough, Neil," she replied loudly. She tapped her foot impatiently, unable to stand still with the adrenaline pumping through her. "Not after what I've been through."

"Or the Doberman could have gone for his throat," Dr. Winn said, as though trying to make her feel better. "Some of these dogs are killers."

The door opened, and the nurse Katie had spoken with moments earlier stepped in, clearly shaken. "Patients are beginning to complain about the yelling going on in here, and I've got a three-year-old in room one who's pitching a temper tantrum and refuses to take a tetanus injection. I tell you, Dr. Winn, I can't take any more."

Katie tossed a look of annoyance her way. "Hellooo? We've got a crisis going on in here, and we don't have time to deal with *your* stress right now."

Dr. Winn patted the nurse on the shoulder. "Call security, please."

An hour later Katie and Neil left the emergency room, escorted by a security guard. Neil was still groggy from the pain medication as an orderly helped him from a wheelchair into the front seat of Katie's car. She held his medication and follow-up sheet with the address of the chiropractor he was supposed to see first thing in the morning.

Katie glanced at the guard who, big as he was, could have been a professional wrestler. "Is this going on my police record? Will I have to be fingerprinted?"

"No, ma'am," he said kindly. "You just need to stay calm and leave the premises."

"It's not her fault," Neil said. "She's pregnant, and she tends to overreact."

"I most certainly do not overreact!" Katie replied.

"Ma'am, are you planning to have your baby at this hospital?" the guard asked.

"Why, yes, as a matter of fact, I am."

He walked away, shaking his head.

Neil looked over at Katie as she climbed into the car and started the engine. "You look pretty in your exercise outfit."

"Don't talk to me," she said.

His head fell against the seat. It was all he could do to keep his eyes open. "I'm sorry, Katie. Next time I promise I'll try to catch a bullet straight through the heart."

"That's not funny. Just go to sleep."

By the time they arrived home, Katie had calmed down. She had, once again, made a public spectacle of herself. When the captain had called, she'd assumed the worst. She had overreacted, just as Neil had said. What was wrong with her?

Katie parked the car and cut the engine. "Wake up, Neil. We're home."

He opened his eyes. "Are you still mad at me?"

She sighed as she opened her door and climbed out. "No, I'm mad at myself."

It was no easy task getting Neil out of the car and into the house. Bruno leaped on Neil the minute they walked through the door. "Down, boy!" Katie ordered. The dog whimpered, tucked his tail and backed away. Neil was falling asleep again. "Let's get you to bed now," she said, prodding him in that direction. He was a big man; it was like moving a mountain.

Once she got him in bed, she allowed Bruno to climb up beside him. He sniffed Neil all over, as if trying to figure out the problem. Finally he looked at Katie. "He hurt his back," she said, "but he'll be okay." She sighed. Now she was talking to dogs.

Her tone of voice must have calmed the animal because Bruno sank beside Neil, plopping his head on Neil's chest, folding one paw over the other. Katie untied Neil's sneakers and tossed them to the floor before she tried to wrestle him out of his jeans. Bruno watched. By the time she was finished, she was out of breath. She stared at Neil, wishing she hadn't been so hard on him.

Seemed like she spent her life waiting for the other shoe to drop, so to speak.

Katie took a five-minute shower, climbed into a pair of boxer-shorts pajamas and grabbed her purse, where she had stuffed Neil's pain pills and muscle relaxants. He wasn't due for anything for four hours. She set the alarm clock in his bedroom so she could give him his next dose when it was time. She turned off the light and climbed in bed. Neil and Bruno were snoring softly. Neil must've sensed her presence because he shifted on the bed.

"Katie?"

"Yes, Neil?"

"I was mizerble without you."

"Me, too."

"I did a lot of…thinking."

She waited. He had dozed off again. She tried to make

herself comfortable on the bed. How she would ever sleep after all that had happened was beyond her.

"Katie?"

"Yes?"

"I luff you. I really do."

She felt her heart swell inside her chest. Tears sprang to her eyes. It took a moment for her to gather her emotions. "I love you, too, Neil. I just wish we weren't so afraid."

The only response was the sound of steady breathing that told her he had finally fallen asleep.

Katie took off work the following week so she could drive Neil to the chiropractor's office each morning. He complained, saying the visits only made the pain worse, but Katie assured him it would get better. "It wouldn't hurt as much if you took a pain pill," she said.

"I don't need pain pills."

"So stop grumbling, superhero."

"What I need is a massage."

"I'll call a massage therapist."

He just looked at her.

Ten minutes later Neil was stripped down to his boxers, Katie straddling his hips, rubbing oil into the lower back muscles along his vertebra. This should not be happening, she told herself, knowing how she reacted to Neil's body. Her own body was so tense she thought her nerves would snap. His hips were taut, his broad back and shoulders fascinating as muscles rippled beneath her touch.

This should not be happening.

"Aw, Katie Lee, you have magic fingers," he said on a sigh. "But then I already know that."

She tried to ignore the sexual undertones. "Are you sure I'm not too heavy?" She was a bit self-conscious because of the weight she'd gained over the past month. She was beginning to feel as big as a pickup truck.

"You're not too heavy. You feel good."

He felt pretty good himself, she thought, wishing she didn't have to actually sit on him to give him the massage. The lower part of her body was reacting in ways it shouldn't, and this was not part of her plan.

She had decided to back off. It was for her own good, she kept telling herself. But it was not easy to do when Neil needed her help at the moment.

Perhaps she should rent a massage table.

Neil grinned to himself as Katie kneaded the muscles in his back. He'd felt her squirm a couple of times and hoped the contact was turning her on as much as it was him. Each time she shifted against him, he closed his eyes and let his mind run amok. He was hard.

After twenty minutes or so Katie's fingers ached. "That's it for now," she said, climbing off him. Not only did her hands and fingers need a break, she had to pull herself together. The last, absolute last, thing she should be doing was straddling Neil Logan's behind!

Back off, Katie, she reminded herself.

Dave and Marjorie visited, as did June and Richard, bringing food and groceries since much of Katie's time was taken up looking after Neil. Calls poured in, including one from Captain Burns who apologized to Katie profusely for scaring her.

"I overreacted," she confessed.

"You're new to this, Katie. I should have been a little more diplomatic about how I broke the news, but everything was coming down at once. The guys moved in quickly and did one helluva job. They put a killer behind bars, and they have enough evidence to keep him there for the rest of his life."

Once again Katie felt herself beaming with pride over what Neil and the other detectives had accomplished.

By the end of the week, and five visits to the chiropractor, Neil's condition had improved. He was up and around. As for Katie, she was exhausted. She was sitting on the sofa reading a book when Neil came into the room.

"I'm bored."

She glanced up. "Why don't you watch TV or read a book?"

"I'm lonely, too."

"I'm in no mood to play Monopoly or chess, Neil." She suspected he had more on his mind than board games, but she was determined to maintain her distance. "I'm relaxing."

He suddenly looked remorseful. "I've been too much trouble."

"You were injured and needed help. You would have done the same for me. You *have* done the same for me."

"How are you feeling?"

"A little tired. The baby is kicking like crazy. Wakes me in the middle of the night."

"No kidding."

"It's kicking right now." She had specifically asked the doctor not to tell her the sex of the baby when she'd undergone the amniocentesis because she wanted to enjoy the surprise.

"May I feel?"

Katie took his hand and placed it near the side of her belly. "Hold on." They waited. "There it is, that little thumping."

Neil's eyes widened as he felt the movement inside. "That's incredible!"

"What's incredible is listening to its heartbeat when I visit the doctor."

"This is pretty exciting, Katie." He had seen the changes on the outside, but he hadn't spent much time thinking about what was going on inside her. Now he was intrigued. "Do you have a book that actually shows all this?"

Neil sat in awe the first hour, looking at pictures and reading sections on the development of an unborn child from a book entitled *The Miracle of Pregnancy.*

"This is fascinating," he said. Once again, he placed his hand on her belly. "I wish the baby were mine."

Katie felt her jaw drop. "What?"

"In a way, it feels like it," he went on, thinking out loud. "I've been with you through most of it."

She looked at him. She suspected he didn't remember telling her he loved her. Or it could have been the effects of the medication he'd been taking at the time. "You've been very kind, Neil."

"It wasn't kindness, Katie." He took her hand in his and studied it. "You know there's more to it than that. I'm in love with you."

Katie felt something inside quicken with those simple words. He'd said it. He'd put his cards on the table, and the look on his face told her he was waiting for her reaction. She was lost as to how to respond. She decided the truth was the only way.

"I love you, too, Neil," she said softly and saw the relief in his eyes, "but I'm afraid."

"Because of my job," he said. He gave her a sad smile. "I saw how you reacted at the hospital."

She blushed. "I made a fool of myself."

"No, Katie. It showed me how much you care for me. It felt good. Until later, when I realized what a price you'd paid emotionally. I don't expect you to live like that no matter how much I care about you."

"What are you saying?"

"Maybe you'd be better off without me."

Her heart wrenched. The thought of being without Neil was so disturbing she couldn't think for a moment. In fact, she thought she might be ill. All the warmth seemed to leave the room, and a chill crept inside her and made her shiver. "I don't know what to say."

Neil was quiet for a moment. "I do," he said. "I'd say we're both pretty pathetic. We're so afraid when it comes to falling in love because we can't bear the thought of something happening."

"We both fear loss," she almost whispered.

"I didn't realize the extent of your fear until that night in the emergency room. You always seemed so strong and confident, proud and determined. Like you owned the world," he added.

"What about you? You're this tough-guy cop who always seems to have everything under control. So cool under pressure."

He gave her a slip of a smile. "We're both good actors." His look turned serious. "Living with fear is no life at all, Katie, and I've spent almost half my life living that way."

"Because of Ryan?"

He nodded. He sighed. "I thought I'd lost it, Katie. I honest to God did not think I would come out of it."

"I know you were in a lot of pain, Neil. We all worried for you."

He continued to hold her hand. "I should have wrestled the keys from him that night," he said, "but Ryan convinced me he was sober enough to drive. Once we got on the road, I could tell he was in no condition so I told him repeatedly to pull over."

"He refused."

"Yeah. And paid for it with his life."

"You paid, too."

"I used to have terrible nightmares," he confessed. "They slip up on me now and then, but in the beginning I was afraid to close my eyes. I kept seeing the accident over and over in my mind, and I could literally feel the sensations I felt that night, the sheer terror only seconds before the crash, the sound of metal crunching and glass bursting from the windows. Then silence. I think that was the worst part."

He paused for a moment and wiped his brow with his free hand. He was sweating. "I must've been unconscious for a moment, but when I woke up, there was that awful silence where all you can hear is the beating of your own heart. I called out to Ryan a number of times before he answered. We were both trapped. There was a full moon that night, so I was able to see the damage. The impact of hitting the tree sent part of the engine into the car. It was sitting in Ryan's lap. To this day, I don't know how I escaped it.

"I knew he was in serious condition. I began asking him questions, forcing him to answer. Somehow I had the presence of mind to hit the flashers, but all I could think to do was keep him talking. I was still talking ninety-to-nothing when they cut us out of the car and pulled Ryan's body out. At least that's what I was later told by the officer who arrived first on the scene. It was pure gibberish. They had to knock me out to shut me up." He offered her a wry smile.

"Then you didn't speak for days."

He pondered it. "You've heard of the black hole, right? It happens when a star burns out and collapses within itself. It's supposed to have some kind of intense gravitational pull." When Katie nodded, he went on. "I've been there. Except the hole was inside of me, and the more I tried to climb out, the deeper I was sucked back into it. If it hadn't been for that cop visiting me in the hospital so much after the accident, I probably would still be there. But he refused to give up on me. He kept telling me there was a reason I lived through the accident. That's when I decided to join the police force."

Katie knew a cop had gotten involved with Neil. He'd

been the first to arrive at the scene. Somehow he'd managed to pull Neil out of the depression. "Do you ever see him?"

Neil smiled at her. "His name is Archer Burns. Captain Archer Burns."

Katie felt an odd prickling sensation along the nape of her neck. The coincidence was startling. "I never knew."

He nodded. "I can never repay him for what he did."

"That's where you're wrong, Neil. You've been paying since the night Ryan died." He looked at her questioningly. "When your partner got hit, you blamed yourself."

"You know about that?"

"Yes. And I know you spent hours and hours at the hospital. I also know you sent the Hendersons five-thousand dollars to cover some of their bills after Jim got hurt."

"Marjorie said something." He didn't look pleased.

Katie shook her head. "The Hendersons told me the first time they called."

"Do you think it was wrong of me?"

"No. I was touched when I heard, but I hope you sent it for the right reason. If you did it out of guilt—" She paused, waiting for an answer. There was none forthcoming. "Don't you see? You're still paying for what happened more than fifteen years ago. You've paid by not allowing anyone to get close to you. You're hell-bent on protecting the world, making a difference, but only from a distance, because you're afraid to let it get personal like it did with Ryan. And you know what? It's never going to be enough until you let go.

"You're not going back to that black hole because you have more experience, more coping skills than you did at twenty. If you didn't, you would never be able to live through some of the things you see on a day-to-day basis."

Neil was quiet for a moment. "What about you?" he asked. "Are you willing to let go?"

"I'm trying, Neil, I really am. It's not easy."

"Because of my line of work. I know. But it's up to you, Katie."

Eleven

The week of Christmas brought with it several parties. Archer Burns and wife, Betty, had a drop-in, and Katie finally met the Hendersons. Teresa was a warm and personable woman who kept seeing to the needs of her husband. Instead of looking worried or tired, she was thrilled to get out of the house and spend the holidays with her favorite people. Katie liked her upbeat attitude.

"How did you ever pull through it all?" she asked the woman.

Teresa shrugged. "You simply do what you have to do when something like this happens. Life has its risks, but it only makes us stronger when times are hard. Our family has grown so much closer. We don't take one another for granted, that's for sure." She paused. "So something good came out of it."

Katie pondered her words the rest of the evening.

June Logan had always gone all-out for the holidays, and

this year was no exception. The house had been decorated from top to bottom, and the smell of pastries and pies filled the air. Katie shopped frantically for last-minute gifts, even though it was hard on her. She was about to enter her eighth month of pregnancy, and it was all she could do to get around. Neil took over the cleaning, cooking and grocery shopping. If he saw Katie standing, he told her to sit. He gave her back rubs and foot rubs, refused to let her pick up anything heavier than a book and constantly asked how she felt.

"I must look pretty bad for you to keep asking me that question," she said one evening.

"You look...very pregnant. I don't know why you keep working."

"I've slowed down. I'm spending more time in my office these days, and the temporary girl is working out fine." Genna had put her foot down after Thanksgiving and insisted it was time to hire someone to work through the holidays and take over once Katie went on maternity leave.

Katie had finally decided what she would give Neil. She bought him a nice watch, exchanging the gold band for leather. She had bought a pair of running shoes, and a new blue jean jacket to replace the one that looked as though it belonged in a Goodwill box. They exchanged gifts Christmas morning with June and Richard, and it was obvious Neil like his gifts. When she opened his, she was stunned to find a diamond-and-sapphire tennis bracelet.

June took a close look at it. "You chose well," she told her son. "The stones are perfect."

The caterer arrived early. Neil was thankful his mother had asked for a traditional Christmas dinner: baked ham, turkey and stuffing, and all the fixings, instead of the usual stuffed goose or pheasant. Afterward they teased Neil of being henpecked when, each time Katie needed something, he jumped to do her bidding. Katie insisted she was pregnant, not helpless, but everyone refused to let her do for herself. When June asked, once again, if Katie had decided what to name the baby, Katie was vague. She had picked out names long before, but she wanted it to be a surprise.

"Just as long as she promises not to name him after Drew," Richard grumbled. A hush fell over the room. "Did I say something wrong?" he asked his wife.

"No, honey, you're far too sensitive to do something like that."

Katie and Neil smiled at each other. They never thought of the baby in connection with Drew. Genna had heard he and his new wife had recently moved to Virginia where her father owned several jewelry stores, and Katie hoped that was the case. Not that it truly mattered. Drew was out of her life, and she had no regrets.

June packed half the leftovers into plastic containers, insisting Neil and Katie take them home so they wouldn't have to cook over the next couple of days. Although the Logans were holding a New Year's Eve bash and had invited half of Atlanta, Neil and Katie told them they planned to spend a quiet evening at home watching the hoopla on TV.

The big night found Katie and Neil exactly where they'd said they would be. Much to Katie's surprise, Neil had ordered a small party platter, complete with vegetables and dip and meat and cheese. He'd even picked up hats and horns. Katie lay on a pillow on the sofa, her feet in Neil's lap, napping on and off as he channel-surfed with the volume low. She fell asleep, only to be awakened with a soft kiss from Neil as the new year rolled in.

Katie awoke the following morning to bad news. Genna had come down with the flu, which meant Katie was going to have to cover for her until Genna recovered. Since Katie's childbirth classes were due the following Monday, only two days away, she had no coach.

Neil saw the disappointment in Katie's eyes when she hung up the phone.

"I can fill in until Genna's better," he offered.

"I have to go two nights a week. Monday and Wednesday."

"No problem."

"They're probably going to show a graphic video of births."

He tossed her a look. "Hey, this is me you're talking to. I've seen it all."

June phoned Katie shortly after she arrived home from work the following day. "Honey, is Neil in?"

"He should be here shortly. Anything I can do for you?"

The woman sighed. "Richard and I were trying to get a box from the attic, and he hurt his back," she said. "I was trying to find Neil's baby blankets for you. Some of them were gifts from his grandparents that I saved, and I want you to have them."

Katie was touched. "Is Richard going to be okay?"

"Yes, he just pulled a muscle."

Neil walked through the front door. "Hold on, June."

He took the phone and listened. "I had an okay day," he said. "Just tired." He frowned. "You need help getting a box out of the attic? What, *now*? Mom, can't this wait?" he asked sharply, earning a dark look from Katie.

She took the phone from Neil. "June, of course we'll help. See you shortly."

They were on their way a few minutes later, Neil grumbling about how tired he was. Katie ignored him. When they pulled into the Logans' driveway, she looked at him. "Now, you be nice," she said.

June met them at the back door. "Oh, thank goodness

you're here. Come on in, the box is this way. But first, let's go and check on Richard. He's in the living room.''

They followed June through the kitchen and butler's pantry, past the dining room into the living room where a group of women yelled, ''Surprise!''

Katie stood there for a moment, eyes blinking. All her friends were there except for Genna. She was glad to see Marjorie and Teresa had made it, as well as Doris and some of her customers from the store. Pink and blue balloons filled with helium nudged the ceiling, their silver and white streamers adding to the festive occasion. A table draped in white held an assortment of dainty sandwiches, pastries and a cake with a plastic baby, diaper and all, leaning forward as though he had just discovered his toes. A selection of nuts, pastel mints and June's prized punch sat on a smaller table. On the folding table next to it was a mountain of gifts, beside it, a stroller, a baby swing and a car seat. A surprise baby shower! She looked at Neil. ''Did you know about this?''

He grinned. ''Why do you think I gave my mother such a hard time about coming over to help her? I knew it would get a rise out of you, and you'd insist on coming with me to see that I behaved myself.''

Katie shook her head sadly. ''You'll stoop to anything, won't you, Logan?'' She looked at Richard. ''So, you're not really hurt?''

He shook his head. ''I've never felt better.'' He got up from the chair. ''As a matter of fact, Neil and I are going out for a sandwich and a cold beer while you ladies carry on.''

Neil looked shocked. The two men had not done anything together in years. He was still wearing a stunned expression as they headed out the door.

Katie and June exchanged looks and shrugged. ''Thank

you so much for doing this for me," Katie said, hugging the woman tightly. "I never suspected."

"I couldn't have done it without Doris and Genna's help," June replied. "They gave me most of the names and addresses of whom I should invite. Genna was so sorry she couldn't make it, but she's terrified of passing on her germs." June clapped her hands together. "Okay, ladies, let's party."

Neil and his father stepped inside a local pub some minutes later and sat down. The place was dead except for a couple sitting at a table near the back. They took a seat at the bar and ordered a beer and a sandwich. "How long do you think this baby shower will last?" Neil asked.

Richard shrugged. "You get a bunch of women in one room, and there's no telling."

They sipped in silence for a moment. "How's the magazine going?" Neil asked.

His father shrugged. "Same as always. We've decided to devote the March issue to crime in the city. I was sort of hoping you'd allow us to interview you, now that you're this big hero."

Neil was touched that his father thought enough of his expertise to get the information he wanted. "I'd be happy to."

"How come you didn't tell me you saved that little boy's life?"

"Oh, that happened some months back."

"Your risked your own life."

"I was just doing my job, Dad. Anybody would have reacted that way."

Their sandwiches arrived. The two men talked about sports and the magazine. Neil began to fidget. "Uh, Dad, I know you'd always hoped that I'd come to work for you," he said, "but I was too hardheaded to appreciate what you were offering me." His father took a sip of his beer and listened, something he rarely did in Neil's growing-up days. Richard Logan had always done the talking; others listened. "I've been doing a lot of thinking lately, what with Katie and the baby to consider, and I was wondering if you still had a place for me there."

Richard wiped his mouth on a napkin, his eyes never leaving his son's face. "I don't know what to say," he replied. "I thought you were happy doing what you're doing. You're certainly making more of a difference in the world than I am."

Neil was taken aback by his response. It was the closest thing to a compliment his father had ever given him. He had waited years for the man's approval, and now that he had it he didn't know what to do with it. "I could still make a difference with the magazine," he said. "I know this town inside out. You're saying you want to print an entire issue on the crime in this city. Why not offer a monthly column on crime? I could fill volumes with what I've learned from the force. I could do a segment on how senior citizens can protect themselves, how parents could better protect their children, what to look for if you suspect you're being conned and—"

"Slow down, Neil," his father said, chuckling. "I've never seen such exuberance. Of course you have a place with the magazine. The damn thing is yours as far as I'm concerned, although I've always suspected you'd sell it and donate the money to some charity after I died. I didn't realize I'd raised such a frugal son. And one so devoted to helping others." He paused. "Neil, you wouldn't last a week with the magazine."

"I'd give it my best shot."

Richard pulled out one of the specialty cigars Katie and Neil had given him for Christmas. He motioned for the bartender. "Do you care if I light this?"

The bartender glanced around. "Don't look like it's going to bother anybody. Go ahead."

Richard lit it and took a puff. "Nothing like a fine cigar. When you get to be my age you'd be amazed at the little things that bring you pleasure." He studied his son. "Did I ever tell you that at one time I wanted to be a lawyer?" When Neil shook his head, he went on. "Oh, I had it all planned. I would attend Columbia University or Harvard, and I would be the best damn trial lawyer money could buy."

"What happened?"

"The family didn't need a lawyer. They needed someone to run a magazine, and my father was not someone you said no to. So, I went to college and graduated with honors as I was expected to do, just so I could start working in the mail room."

"The mail room?"

"The old man didn't want to show favoritism. I had to prove myself." He took another puff of his cigar. "No matter how hard I worked, no matter that I was heir to the magazine, it took me two years to get out of that mail room. And guess what I did down there when I wasn't busy?" He didn't wait for an answer. "I read law books." He chuckled. "That's why I'm always ready to sue someone if they cross me. I know more about law than most attorneys."

"I never knew."

Richard motioned for another round. "So you can imagine how I felt when you informed me you had no desire to take over the magazine because you planned to be a cop."

Neil glanced down. "You must've hated me."

"Not at all. I was mad as hell. Took me a long time to get over it. But I was mad as hell because you followed your dreams and I didn't. At the same time, I respected your determination, and when I realize how much of a difference you're making in this world—'' He paused. "Well, I feel so proud I don't know what to say."

"All these years I've felt like a big disappointment to you."

"I should have told you differently, son, but I've never really been able to express my feelings like a lot of people. If I seemed disappointed, it was at myself for not standing up to my father as I should have."

Neil had never known the man to be so blatantly open and honest. "Katie doesn't like me being a cop," he said. "I know this marriage started out as a way to protect her and the baby, but I want it to be real. That's not going to happen as long as I'm on the force." He went on to tell him how Katie had reacted to his recent injury.

"Katie's mother was yanked from her when the girl was too young to cope with something of that magnitude. She's a grown woman now, and she's strong. If you give up what you love doing, you'll begin to resent her. As hard as it sounds, she's going to have to learn to deal with fear and insecurity like the rest of us. You'll be doing her a great favor, Neil."

Neil was still pondering his father's words as he and Katie drove home that night, his Jeep filled to the brim with gifts. Katie had fallen asleep as soon as they'd started down the road. As much as he loved her, as much as he wanted her and the baby in his life, he could not give up that part of himself that made him the man he was. He could not protect her from the realities of life any more than he could protect himself.

He'd learned that lesson the hard way, by shutting himself off, by refusing to get close to those who loved him most. There was pain in the world, simple as that. The loss of a loved one was devastating. But he had discovered there was more pain in not opening himself to love.

If only Katie would take that chance.

* * *

Neil shuddered against the January chill and checked the address in his hand. It was Saturday, and he had the day off. He would have preferred sleeping late, but he had things to do. He knocked on the front door of a medium-size frame house that looked as though it had been painted recently. Azalea bushes skirted the house, and a tall elm threw a shadow across the neat lawn. No answer. He knocked again. The woman had promised she would be there. He thought he heard noises coming from the back-yard. He hurried down the porch steps and followed the driveway.

The woman was hanging her wash on the clothesline. Beside her a little boy pulled brightly colored plastic clothespins from a cloth bag. "Mrs. North?" Neil called out.

The woman turned and smiled. "You must be Detective Logan."

Neil nodded and crossed the yard, never taking his eyes off the boy who stared back at him curiously. He finally looked at the woman. "Call me Neil," he said.

"I'm Regina North," she said. "Friends call me Reenie."

"So, you're Bobby's aunt." She was a pretty woman in her early thirties, dressed in jeans and a thick sweater.

She surprised Neil with a hug. "Yes, and I am so happy you called. My family and I have been trying to reach you. We all wanted to thank you for saving Bobby's life, as well as the other detective, Jim Henderson, who tried so hard to reach my mother in time. We were so deeply moved that two people put their own lives on the line to try to protect our loved ones. Our church has been praying for you and Detective Henderson ever since. I hope he's better."

"He's home recuperating now." Neil knew the Norths' church had sent Jim and Teresa a love donation, as they'd called it, to help with the finances during Jim's convalescence. "Please give everyone our thanks for the cards and letters and the donations to the Henderson family, Mrs. North."

"Reenie." She looked at Bobby. "This is that nice policeman who kept you from getting hurt. Do you remember him?"

Bobby nodded. "Peesman?" His eyes were fixed on Neil.

"He probably doesn't understand why you aren't wearing a uniform."

Neil reached inside his jacket and pulled out his badge. "See this, Bobby?" The boy hesitated before touching it, then ran a finger across the top of it.

"Peesman!" he exclaimed.

Neil chuckled, reached into another pocket and brought out a plastic badge the guys sometimes gave kids when they visited schools. Bobby squealed in delight as Neil clipped it to his jacket.

The two adults laughed. "How's he doing?" Neil asked Regina.

She shrugged. "Cried for Mamaw the first couple of nights, but he's okay now. Poor baby. He's certainly had his share of hard times. Fortunately, he's too young to understand."

Neil had checked into Bobby's past. His mother had been sent to a correctional facility when Bobby was six months old, and she was serving a twelve-year sentence for two counts of armed robbery. It explained why his grandmother had been raising him. DSS had placed him, at least temporarily, with his aunt and uncle who adored him, despite having three children of their own.

"He's lucky to have you and your husband," Neil said.

"We consider Bobby a blessing."

"I understand your sister gave you the go-ahead to adopt Bobby."

Reenie nodded. "I think she finally realized how desperately Bobby needs a real home."

"He's a lucky little boy. I'd like to visit, now and then, if you don't mind."

"You're always welcome in our home."

Neil knelt in front of him. "Bobby, how would you like to go out for an ice-cream cone?" The child looked up from his plastic badge and immediately raised his arms to Neil, who swooped him up. Bobby looked at his aunt with a delightful smile. She smiled back, and Neil saw the love in her eyes.

"Mind your manners, young man," she said, giving him a peck of a kiss on his cheek.

Neil swung the boy high on his shoulder and started for his Jeep. He was glad he'd come.

The sun had risen higher in the sky when Neil pulled into the cemetery and drove toward the back. Christmas flowers and wreaths still adorned the graves. Neil parked his Jeep, stepped out and made his way toward a grave where a vase of red flowers stood, surrounded by holly branches.

He looked down at the marker. "Hi, Ryan, it's me," he said. "I'm sorry I haven't stopped by in such a long time, but I thought it was time we talked." Neil got down on his knees. He wondered what his friend would look like now if he were still alive. In his mind, he still saw Ryan as he'd looked at twenty. For a long time Neil just sat there and thought about his friend.

"You're not going to believe this, pal," he said, pulling his jacket together when a sudden wind gusted by, "but I have fallen in love. Yep, you heard me right. Her name is Katie. You remember Katie, don't you? We used to pull terrible tricks on her. You wouldn't recognize her now. She's this tiny little thing—well, she was always a bit of a runt, but she's the most beautiful woman I've ever laid eyes on.

"She's kind, Ryan. I see some of the things people do to one another out there, and some of it's so bad I feel like I don't belong in the human race anymore. And then I look at Katie, and all I can see is this sweet woman who would never hurt a soul, and when she touches me, I—" He paused. "I'm reminded just how many good people there really are out there." Neil tried to straighten the flowers. "There's a baby on the way, too. It isn't mine, but I know I'm going to love him. Or her," he added.

Neil chuckled after a moment, realizing he suddenly sounded twenty-one years old again. That was what love did to a person, he supposed. And it was almost as if Ryan was sitting there giving him that lopsided smile of his, blond hair ruffling in the breeze. "Remember how we swore we'd never get married and have kids? We didn't want to end up like our parents. But once you know it's the right person—" He paused, and his throat grew thick with emotion. "I'm sorry you'll never know what it's like, Ryan, because falling in love is the best thing that ever happened to me." His eyes smarted with tears. "I just want you to be happy for me, I guess, and I know you are because you were always like that." Neil felt a tear slide down his cheek. He never cried, not even the day of Ryan's funeral. Now the tears fell freely.

He sat there as another breeze wafted by. "You know, I've been by to visit you a lot of times over the years. Each time I come I ask you to forgive me. Such a stupid thing to ask since I know you never held it against me in the first place." Neil drew in a shaky breath and swiped at his tears. "But this time I'm asking you to help me forgive myself."

It was nearing dusk by the time Neil stood and headed

for his car. He felt like a new man, as though a giant boulder had been rolled off his shoulders. He owed part of it to Katie. She had changed him forever. He climbed into his car and saw that his cell phone was blinking. He punched a button, and Katie's voice came on.

"Neil, it's me. I don't want to worry you, but I've been experiencing a little pain today, and Genna is driving me to the hospital as I speak." She chuckled. "The woman is wearing a surgical mask over her mouth, if you can believe it. I'm sure everything is okay. My doctor just wants to take a quick look. I'll see you at home later."

Neil frowned. Katie in pain? He didn't like the sound of it. It was too soon for her to be in labor. Wasn't it?

Twelve

——

Arriving at the hospital, Neil barely acknowledged his parents before a nurse escorted him to labor and delivery. He found Katie in bed, Genna standing beside her, wearing her mask. "I'm here, baby," he said, hurrying up to Katie. He took her hand.

She looked frightened. "I'm in labor."

"What does the doctor say?"

As if acting on cue, Dr. Chambers sailed through the door. He gave Neil a quick smile as he washed his hands and slipped on gloves. "Your wife seems to be in a big hurry to have this baby, Mr. Logan."

"Is it safe at this point?"

"I am a little concerned as to whether the baby's lungs are mature enough, but if he shows signs of respiratory distress, we have an excellent neonatal intensive-care unit. He'll be placed in an incubator and monitored around the clock."

"Is there no way to prevent an early delivery?" Katie asked, her anxiety increasing as she thought of the risks involved to her unborn child. "I've read articles—"

Dr. Chambers interrupted by shaking his head. "Katie, with the sack rupturing, there's an increased chance of a serious infection. I'd like to schedule an immediate cesarean section. The baby is not positioned correctly, since he's early. You've been laboring six hours and made absolutely no progress. I could try to induce labor, and I could attempt to turn the baby, but I don't recommend it under the circumstances. The baby is too small and too fragile."

Katie went into a contraction. Neil was not prepared for it, and he watched her suffer through as he tried to remember all he'd learned in the childbirth class. He would be prepared for the next one.

"What do you say?" the doctor asked.

Neil and Katie looked at each other. Neil took her hand. "I don't think we have much of a choice, honey."

She nodded, although reluctantly. "I'll agree to the cesarean section." Genna slipped from the room quietly.

Neil was with Katie when Dr. Chambers delivered a baby boy, but the newborn was whisked away so quickly that neither of them got a look. Neil remained with Katie while she was cleaned up and covered with a warm blanket. A nurse injected something into her IV—it would help with pain, the woman said—and Katie drifted off to sleep, still holding Neil's hand.

When Katie opened her eyes some time later, she discovered it was late. She was groggy, disoriented. Nearby she found Neil slumped into a recliner beside the bed. "Neil?"

He awoke instantly. "What, sweetheart?"

"The baby? How is he?"

"He's doing fine. They've got him in the neonatal unit, snug as a bug in a rug."

"They took him away so quickly. I barely got a look at him."

"The staff is doing everything they can for him, Katie."

"How much did he weigh?"

Neil hesitated. "Close to four pounds."

Her heart wrenched. How could something that tiny survive? She turned her head so Neil could not see the tears in her eyes.

"Try to sleep, babe. We'll know more tomorrow."

Sleep did not come easily, and as the night wore on, Katie's fears only worsened. She dreaded morning, when she would have to face the news.

Katie and Neil were dressed in hospital garb when they met with the staff neonatologist later the next morning. Dr. Susan Chi, a lovely Asian woman with blue-black hair that fell to her lower back, seemed warm and caring as she spoke with them in a conference area. "Baby Logan is doing as well as expected," she said. "He was carefully monitored through the night, and his vital signs look good this morning." She smiled. "I don't like to take new parents back until I've explained what's going on, because it can all be overwhelming at first. This facility is set up so that we can provide the very best in neonatal care," Dr. Chi went on. "We have access to pediatric specialists, and our babies are constantly monitored. I want you both to feel confident that we're doing everything possible for your son."

Neil and Katie nodded and listened. "How does he look?" Katie asked.

"He has been placed in an incubator, as I believe you already know, so we can maintain his body heat and reduce his risk of infections. He is connected to monitors so we can watch his heart rate, blood pressure, body temperature. If your newborn so much as blinks his eyes, we know about it.'' She smiled as if hoping to ease the tension in the room.

''It may appear a little scary at first. We've inserted a tube into his trachea to assist in his breathing, and we're providing liquid nutrition through a feeding tube.''

Katie closed her eyes at the mental picture she was drawing in her mind. Neil took her hand.

''How long will he have to remain in the unit?'' Neil asked.

''It depends on how he responds,'' Dr. Chi replied. She looked at Katie, and her eyes softened. ''Mrs. Logan, we're accustomed to treating very ill babies. Some of them arrive weighing little more than a pound or two. It's amazing what we can do with advanced technology and pediatric specialists. But you and your husband will be a huge benefit to what we're doing. Baby Logan needs you. He needs to hear your voice and feel your touch, and we encourage new parents to spend as much time with their newborns as possible. We'll ask you to use a breast pump so that when Baby Logan is able to tolerate breast milk we'll have it on hand. It takes teamwork, Mrs. Logan.'' She paused. ''Are you ready to see your new son?''

Katie was not exactly prepared for the neonatal unit. A pediatric nurse stood beside her as she gazed at her son for the first time. ''It's okay to reach inside and touch your baby,'' the nurse said. ''He needs to be touched often, and he needs to hear the sound of your voice. You'd be surprised what he's able to recognize at this early age.''

Katie's fingers trembled as she reached through an opening in the incubator and touched her son for the first time, trying to avoid the tubes and wires that sprouted from his tiny body. ''Hi, little one,'' she said. He turned and gazed in her direction, but his face was expressionless. She stroked his leg, and it obviously startled him because he began to cry.

Katie pulled away.

Neil reached inside and stroked the baby's silky skin for the first time. "He's beautiful, Katie," he whispered. "Just like you."

Katie saw no resemblance. The baby that had grown inside her all those months now seemed like a stranger. She felt empty inside.

"Are you okay?" Neil asked here.

"I'm just tired, Neil. So tired."

Flowers began arriving that afternoon. The APD and the detective unit each sent a big bouquet, June and Richard sent a vase of tiny white tea roses and Dave and Marjorie, a potted plant with building blocks in blue and pink. The Logans arrived shortly after Katie returned from the nursery.

"He's the prettiest baby I've ever seen," June declared, "and so healthy-looking for a preemie. Have you named him yet?"

"No. I guess I've been so caught up in everything. And worried," she added, trying to make excuses.

"I'm going to call him Bubba," Neil said teasingly, wishing he could cheer Katie. The smile on her face was forced and didn't reach her eyes.

"A fine boy," Richard said.

Katie knew they were trying to make her feel better. "Thank you," Katie said.

Genna hurried in with a giant teddy bear and declared the baby was the best-looking one in the entire nursery. "He may be small, but you just watch. He'll end up being a linebacker for the high school football team."

That evening Marjorie and Dave stopped by with the Hendersons, all of them bearing gifts. "He looks just like

Neil,'' Marjorie said, bringing a proud smile to Neil's face. Katie and Neil exchanged looks. By the time they all left, Katie was exhausted. She went to bed early.

Dr. Chambers stopped by to check on Katie the next morning, checked her stitches and told her she was doing fine. "Have you been by to see the baby yet?"

"I plan to visit with him later."

He squeezed her hand before he left. He wasn't gone long before Dr. Chi appeared.

"How's he doing?" Katie asked.

The other woman took a seat beside her bed. "I wish I had better news for you this morning, Mrs. Logan, but he's lost a little weight, and he's a bit lethargic. Some of that's to be expected, of course. We've changed his formula, but I suggest you start pumping breast milk right away."

Katie nodded.

"Are you still wrestling with names?" Dr. Chi asked. "Everybody is calling him Baby Logan."

"I have several in mind. I've just had so much on my mind."

"That's understandable. Just hang in there, he'll come around."

Neil was not there to hear the news. When he came in, he found Katie looking depressed. She gave him the news. "I've been using the breast pump as I was told. They've taken what little milk I had over to the neonatal unit."

"Have you seen him yet?"

"No." She turned tearful eyes to him. "I don't want to see him just now, Neil. I'm too afraid."

"He needs you right now. Maybe you should try to put aside your fears for the time being. For his sake."

"I'll visit later. After I've rested."

"Don't do this to yourself, Katie. I know you're frightened, but—"

She turned angry eyes to him. "You don't know what

I'm feeling right now," she snapped. "You have no idea. I carried this baby for eight months. He was supposed to be the family I'd always wanted. I don't want to get attached to him, because I don't know if he's going to live or not."

"That's the most selfish thing I've ever heard come out of your mouth," he said tersely. "This isn't about you, Katie. Your baby needs you right now."

"I can't."

Neil looked disappointed as he turned for the door. "I can't live like this, Katie, always fearing the worst. So your baby is small and has a few problems. It happens, okay? But you're so caught up in your own misery you can't think of him."

"Don't judge me, Neil. You have your own issues."

"And I've dealt with them because I refuse to spend the rest of my life avoiding love. I love you, Katie, more than I've ever loved anyone in my life, but I will not live with a woman who can't love me because she feels there are too many risks involved. A woman who won't reach out to her own baby when he needs her most." Neil shook his head sadly and left without another word.

Katie's heart shattered into so many pieces that she was certain she would never be able to put them all together again.

The chapel was small and plain, a place where those of all denominations could find solace and comfort. Katie took a seat in the back row. She wasn't alone. In the front row a young woman sobbed quietly into a wad of tissues. Katie felt her heart turn over in her chest at the sight, and she wondered what had happened to bring her so much pain.

Katie realized the woman was so lost in grief she had no idea she was there. "Excuse me, ma'am," she whispered. "I don't mean to intrude upon your privacy, but is there anything I can do to help?"

The woman had the saddest eyes Katie had ever seen. It wasn't simply because they were red and swollen, but the despair was almost more than Katie could take. "I appreciate your concern," she said, "but—" She sighed, and the sound seemed to rise from the very depths of her soul. "I just need strength, I guess."

"Do you have a loved one here?"

"A baby. A little girl we named Sissy." She sighed. "I feel guilty spending so much time here. I have two other children who need me. My husband needs me. I can't work right now so he has taken a second job. We have to depend on friends and neighbors to help out." Fresh tears. "Sissy has a lot of problems. I know she's growing stronger every day, but sometimes I feel overwhelmed. I wonder if it will never end or if our lives will ever become normal again."

Katie could truly sympathize. "I have a baby here, also. He was a month early. I'm sure he doesn't have the problems your baby daughter has, but I'm terrified something will happen and he won't pull through. I'm afraid to see him, afraid I'll become attached, only to lose him in the end."

The woman captured Katie's hand. "You need to see your baby," she said gently. "You need to touch him. They say there is nothing like a mother's touch."

"I feel so ashamed," Katie confessed. "Right now it's hard to believe he belongs to me. I never thought I'd feel that way about my own baby."

"It's hard at first. So scary. I felt that way, also. It's normal."

They sat in silence for a moment, two strangers comforting each other. Katie suspected the woman was praying because her mouth moved from time to time as she gazed at the altar. Katie thought of her mother, all the love they'd shared. She had spent close to her entire life focusing on what it had felt like to lose her, when she should have been remembering the fun times they'd had together. And Neil. He had brought so much joy into her life, had shown her the way it should be between a man and a woman, but she had let her worries about his job consume her instead of realizing what a lucky woman she was for being a part of him. That's what she was, a part of him, as though they shared their very souls.

She suddenly realized losing his love would be the biggest loss of all.

And her son, fighting for his life, while she just sat there, afraid to see him in case he didn't pull through. Neil was right. She *was* being selfish. Perhaps she had been selfish all her life. She had thought because she'd lost her mother that life would be kinder to her, that she would be exempt from further pain because she had already paid her dues. She had lost both parents, but she had never stopped to realize how truly blessed she'd been to have June and Richard take her in and love her as their own. Instead she had become fearful, afraid they would get tired of her and put her in a foster home. Wasn't that why she had worked so hard to be the perfect child? But life wasn't always perfect.

Katie continued to sit there until a feeling of peace stole over her. She would be okay. When she finally rose, the woman looked at her, a question in her eyes.

"Thank you for helping me," Katie said. "I'm going to see my baby now." She left the chapel and headed in the direction of the neonatal unit.

Katie felt her heart turn over in her chest when she reached inside the incubator and touched her baby, as if for the first time. He looked at her. She smiled and cooed at him. "Hi, sweetheart," she said softly. "Mommy's here, and I will never leave you again." The baby kicked his legs, and she laughed. "I believe you're excited to see me.

I certainly am excited to see you. And guess what? It won't be long until I can hold you. What do you think about that?''

The baby looked at her. Katie wondered when he had become so beautiful.

A nurse appeared, as if she had come out of nowhere. She introduced herself as Lila Wright. ''You must be feeling better, Mrs. Logan,'' she said.

Katie nodded. ''Much better, thank you.''

''This little boy is going to grow as tall as his father.''

Katie looked at her. ''His father?''

''Mr. Logan has been by several times, but he didn't want to disturb you. Have you come up with a name yet?''

Katie smiled. ''I've decided to call him Richard Neil Logan, after the two finest men I've ever known.''

Dinner arrived, and Katie had still not heard one word from Neil. He was angry with her, and she didn't blame him. That didn't stop her from missing him, wanting him. When a knock came at the door, Katie sat up straighter in the bed and fluffed her hair into place. Instead of Neil, the woman from the chapel peeked in.

''Am I disturbing you?''

''Oh, no. Please come in.''

The woman sat in the chair beside Katie's bed. ''We've never formally met, but I'm Ellen Farmer.''

''Katie Logan.'' They shook hands.

''I want to thank you for sitting with me in the chapel,'' Ellen said. ''You were a big help.''

''You helped me as well. How's Sissy?''

''She's holding her own. She's a fighter.''

''So are we, Ellen.''

The woman nodded. ''Yes, we are.''

Katie was released two days later, and although she hated leaving Richie—the nickname she'd given him—she knew he was in good hands. She called a cab and left with instructions to pump her breast milk and bring it each time she came. She arrived home to an empty house. She checked Neil's room. A feeling of desolation washed over her. Where was he?

For the next few days Katie spent almost every waking hour at the hospital, caring for Richie as much as she could. June and Richard visited often, as did Genna and Marjorie. None of them asked about Neil as they made arrangements to see that Katie was able to get back and forth to the hospital without calling a cab.

"Neil will come around," Genna said, once they were alone.

"It's not Neil's fault," Katie replied, and left it like that.

Richie had begun to put on weight, a few ounces at a time, but he was making progress. Two days later they removed the tubes. Katie came in the next morning and stood beside Dr. Chi as she pulled the baby from the little crib. He cried loudly, and they all laughed. Katie finally held him for the first time, and she thought her heart would burst with joy. She nursed him from her own breast, and the love she felt left her breathless. She wished Neil were there to experience it with her.

She missed him so badly it hurt. She had seen evidence of his comings and goings at the house, but he was doing everything to avoid her. She didn't blame him. She had let her insecurities get in the way. She had not trusted him to take care of himself where his job was concerned. She had asked him to give up a career he loved so she could feel secure, only to discover security came from within.

Richie was released a week later after weighing in at five and a half pounds. Lila Wright helped Katie collect the baby's things. "Where's Daddy?" she asked, referring to Neil. "He was so excited to hear Richie was going home."

Katie blinked back at her. "My, uh, husband called?"

Lila looked surprised. "He calls every day. He's been in a couple of times to check on Richie. Didn't you know?"

Katie tried to hide her embarrassment. "He's working a big case. He hasn't been home much the past few days."

Lila nodded as though it made perfect sense. "Now, here's your appointment card. Richie is scheduled to see his pediatrician day after tomorrow. I've jotted my number down, as well. You can call me anytime."

Katie hugged her and placed Richie into his new car seat, strapping him in carefully. With Genna's help and that of a young orderly, she managed to get everything into the elevator. The elevator door opened to the lobby, and Katie almost bumped into Neil, who was in the process of getting on.

Her heart thundered at the sight of him. She opened her mouth to speak, but the words wouldn't come.

"I heard Richie was being released today," he said. "I thought I'd give you a lift home."

"Genna has already offered."

Genna looked from one to the other. "You know, I just realized I have a lunch date. I'm sorry, Katie."

Katie knew Genna was lying as she rushed out the glass doors.

Outside, Neil helped Katie and Richie into the car before loading their things into the trunk. They made the drive in silence. When they arrived back at Neil's house, he helped them inside and began unloading his Jeep.

"You have messages on the answering machine," he told her. "A real estate agent called saying she found you a place. Don't you think it's a bit early to move a newborn?"

Katie looked away. "I thought it best under the circumstances."

He stepped up to the bassinet. "My dad and I were touched that you named him after us."

"It only seemed fitting."

"He's a cute little guy."

"I think so."

They were making small talk. "Neil, I've been thinking."

He turned to her. "So have I."

"I've acted foolishly. I don't know what got into me."

"You've been through a lot, Katie. I understand."

Did he? "Neil, I've never really been in love until now. It all seemed to happen so fast. I was scared, what with a baby on the way. I know you love me, but Richie's part of my life now, too."

Neil nodded but made no comment.

"The thought of falling in love with a man who spends so much time in a dangerous world scared the hell out of me, but I've done a lot of growing up over the past couple of weeks. I thought I was going to lose my baby, but I realized that even if he hadn't pulled through, I would rather have suffered the pain of losing than never to have known him at all or held him in my arms.

"You can walk away from me right now, Neil, and I wouldn't blame you one bit. I never wanted to be a burden to you. I know it will hurt if you decide you don't want Richie and me in your life, but I'll get through it." She smiled ruefully. "I may be a runt, but I'm tougher than I look."

"You were never a burden, Katie. You changed my life. I don't want to lose you." He stepped closer. "You gave me the courage to face the things in my life that needed to be taken care of so I *could* love you the way you deserved to be loved. I don't ever want to shut myself off from the

world again. I want us to be a real family. I want to adopt
Richie. I may not be his biological father, but I will love
him as my own son."

"He'll have to know the truth someday."

"I know that. But I'm hoping by then he'll know he has
a family who loves him and will stand by him no matter
what. I'm hoping he will have brothers and sisters by then,
but I will swear to you right now that I'll love him as much
as I will the children we create together."

Katie's heart was bursting with love for the man in front
of her, a man who claimed she had changed his life. She
wondered if he had any idea how he'd changed hers. "I
don't know what to say," she confessed, "except I feel
blessed to have you in my life. I don't care what tomorrow
brings. I'm willing to risk it all." She paused. "You're a
good cop, Neil. I wish I had trusted you more."

He reached out for her and pulled her into his arms.
"You don't know what that means to me." He kissed her
softly on the lips. When he raised his head, the look in his
eyes was intense. "I want to renew our vows, Katie. I want
a real marriage. What do you say?"

"Your mother won't like it. She's already given me two
weddings in less than a year."

He laughed. "She thrives on that sort of thing. It'll give
her a chance to pull out her fine china. What do you say?
Will you marry me?"

"There's only one answer to that question. Yes."

Once again he held her close, wondering why it had
taken him so long to realize he and Katie belonged together.
They continued to hold each other, and Katie knew they
had both found peace at last. They had let go of the past
and found a future with each other.

They could be a real family now.

* * * * *

If you liked this romance,
be sure to watch for

HOT SHOT

by Charlotte Hughes,
coming only to Mira in September.

And now for a sneak preview,
please turn the page.

One

Police chief Matt Webber watched as a late-model Nissan pulled in front of the property and parked. A woman climbed out and peered over the top of the car. At first she just stared.

"Oh my God!" she cried out. "Please tell me this isn't four-one-four Elm Street."

Matt walked toward her. She wasn't from Purdyville— he would have noticed her. "May I help you?"

"Is this four-one-four Elm?"

"Yes, it is."

Frankie slapped her open palm against her forehead. "Aw, shit!"

Matt shoved his hands in his pockets and exchanged glances with Orvell. "Is there something I can do for you, Miss?"

Frankie turned to Orvell and noted his uniform, which indicated he was with the fire department. "What happened here?"

"House burned down."

Frankie sighed and rolled her eyes. "I've already figured that out for myself. How did it happen?"

"We suspect arson."

"Aw, damn. Damn, damn, damn!"

Matt chuckled. As much as he liked pretty women—and this one was easy on the eyes—her language made him think of truck stops and bus stations.

Frankie eyed the tall, dark-haired man and wondered what he looked like beneath the grime and soot. Not that she had any business looking at men, after what she'd been through. "You think this is funny?"

Matt closed the distance between them. She looked mad enough to chew a fence post. He crossed his arms and leaned against the woman's car. "No, I don't think it's a dang bit funny, lady, but there's not much sense in cryin' over spilled milk, as they say. You mind telling me why you're in such a tizzy?"

Frankie would have told him to mind his own business if she weren't so upset. "I was supposed to rent this place. I've driven for hours, I'm exhausted—"

"And irritable," Matt supplied, and received a dark look.

"And now I have no place to live. Well, that's just dandy. Would you mind not leaning on my car? You're getting it filthy, and I just washed and waxed it."

Matt stepped away, noting where the soot from his jeans had smudged her automobile. "Sorry about that. Guess I'm a little on the tired side myself." He wiped the car with his palm, and the smudge grew worse.

"Now look what you've done," Frankie said in exasperation. She felt the beginnings of a headache. "Just leave it alone, okay?"

"No way," Matt said. "I'm not about to dirty up your car. Fine lady like you shouldn't have to ride around with soot all over the side of her vehicle. Orvell, you got a clean handkerchief?"

The man pulled one out of his pants pocket and handed it to Matt, who managed to get most of the grime off. "There now, that's better. I can always borrow the neighbor's hose and wash it if you like."

"That won't be necessary." Frankie didn't like his attitude. As if she didn't have enough problems, she had to run into some smart-mouthed hillbilly who seemed hell-bent on making the situation worse.

"I meant no disrespect," Matt said. "Just trying to be friendly. You look like you could take my head off my shoulders with one bite."

"I reckon she's under a lot of stress," Orvell said, "just arriving in town to find her rental house burned down and all."

"Stress?" Frankie asked. "I invented the word. But you needn't make excuses for my behavior. I'm a grown woman, and a professional police detective." She motioned toward the house. "This is child's play compared to what I've seen."

Orvell started to say something, but Matt interrupted. "A real police detective, huh? Well, I'm impressed. How about you, Orvell?"

He gave Matt a funny look. "Yeah."

"And a damn good one at that," Frankie replied, unaware of the looks the men were giving one another.

"So, what brings you to Purdyville?" Orvell asked.

"Job transfer. I'm going to be working for the Purdyville Police Department. And believe me, it won't be easy working with a bunch of good ol' boys after the pros I've dealt with. What can you tell me about the police chief?"

Matt and Orvell exchanged amused looks. "Oh, well, he's a nice enough guy," Matt said. "Good-looking, too."

The other man chuckled. "And don't think he don't know it. Why, half the women in town are hot for him."

"A ladies' man, huh?" Frankie snorted. "Just what I need. Another man whose brain is located behind his zipper."

Matt frowned. Orvell roared with laughter.

"Did I say something funny?" Frankie asked.

"Lady, I don't know you personally," Orvell managed,

"but I hate to just stand here and watch you dig yourself into a deep hole."

"It's okay," Matt said. "I'm enjoying myself."

Frankie sensed they were making fun of her. "Would the two of you mind sharing your little joke with me? I'm in no mood to play guessing games."

Orvell stepped forward. "I'd like to introduce you to Purdyville's esteemed police chief, Matt Webber."

The color drained from Frankie's face as she met Webber's amused gaze. His eyes were a startling blue. She simply stared, mortified by her own behavior.

"I think she's speechless," Orvell said.

Silhouette Desire

presents

DYNASTIES:
THE CONNELLYS

A brand-new miniseries about the Connellys of Chicago,
a wealthy, powerful American family tied by blood to the
royal family of the island kingdom of Altaria.
They're wealthy, powerful and rocked by
scandal, betrayal...and passion!

Look for a whole year of glamorous and
utterly romantic tales in 2002:

Silhouette®

Where love comes alive™

Visit Silhouette at www.eHarlequin.com   SDDYN02

*A powerful earthquake
ravages Southern California...*

*Thousands are trapped
beneath the rubble...*

*The men and women of
Morgan Trayhern's team
face their most heroic
mission yet...*

A brand-new series from
USA TODAY bestselling author

LINDSAY McKENNA

Don't miss these breathtaking
stories of the triumph of love!

Look for one title per month
from each Silhouette series:

August: THE HEART BENEATH
(Silhouette Special Edition #1486)

September: RIDE THE THUNDER
(Silhouette Desire #1459)

October: THE WILL TO LOVE
(Silhouette Romance #1618)

**November: PROTECTING
HIS OWN**
(Silhouette Intimate Moments #1185)

*Available at your favorite
retail outlet*

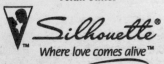

Visit Silhouette at www.eHarlequin.com   SXSMMUR

eHARLEQUIN.com

community | membership

buy books | authors | online reads | magazine | learn to write

buy books

♥ We have your favorite books from Harlequin, Silhouette, MIRA and Steeple Hill, plus bestselling authors in Other Romances. Discover savings, find new releases and fall in love with past classics all over again!

online reads

♥ Read daily and weekly chapters from Internet-exclusive serials, and decide what should happen next in great interactive stories!

magazine

♥ Learn how to spice up your love life, play fun games and quizzes, read about celebrities, travel, beauty and so much more.

authors

♥ Select from over 300 author profiles and read interviews with your favorite bestselling authors!

community

♥ Share your passion for love, life and romance novels in our online message boards!

learn to write

♥ All the tips and tools you need to craft the perfect novel, including our special romance novel critique service.

membership

♥ FREE! Be the first to hear about all your favorite themes, authors and series and be part of exciting contests, exclusive promotions, special deals and online events.

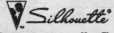

Silhouette®

Where love comes alive™—online...

Visit us at
www.eHarlequin.com

SINT7CH

If you enjoyed what you just read,
then we've got an offer you can't resist!

Take 2 bestselling
love stories FREE!
Plus get a FREE surprise gift!

Clip this page and mail it to Silhouette Reader Service™

IN U.S.A.
3010 Walden Ave.
P.O. Box 1867
Buffalo, N.Y. 14240-1867

IN CANADA
P.O. Box 609
Fort Erie, Ontario
L2A 5X3

YES! Please send me 2 free Silhouette Desire® novels and my free surprise gift. After receiving them, if I don't wish to receive anymore, I can return the shipping statement marked cancel. If I don't cancel, I will receive 6 brand-new novels every month, before they're available in stores! In the U.S.A., bill me at the bargain price of $3.57 plus 25¢ shipping and handling per book and applicable sales tax, if any*. In Canada, bill me at the bargain price of $4.24 plus 25¢ shipping and handling per book and applicable taxes**. That's the complete price and a savings of at least 10% off the cover prices—what a great deal! I understand that accepting the 2 free books and gift places me under no obligation ever to buy any books. I can always return a shipment and cancel at any time. Even if I never buy another book from Silhouette, the 2 free books and gift are mine to keep forever.

225 SDN DNUP
326 SDN DNUQ

Name	(PLEASE PRINT)	
Address	Apt.#	
City	State/Prov.	Zip/Postal Code

* Terms and prices subject to change without notice. Sales tax applicable in N.Y.
** Canadian residents will be charged applicable provincial taxes and GST.
All orders subject to approval. Offer limited to one per household and not valid to current Silhouette Desire® subscribers.
® are registered trademarks of Harlequin Books S.A., used under license.

DES02   ©1998 Harlequin Enterprises Limited

Have you ever wanted to participate in a romance reading group?

Silhouette Special Edition's exciting new book club!

Don't miss

RYAN'S PLACE
by Sherryl Woods

coming in September

Get your friends or relatives together to engage in lively discussions with the suggested reading group questions provided at the end of the novel. Also, visit www.readersring.com for more reading group information!

Available at your favorite retail outlet.

Where love comes alive™

SSEBC1

COMING NEXT MONTH

#1459 RIDE THE THUNDER—Lindsay McKenna
Morgan's Mercenaries: Ultimate Rescue
Lieutenant Nolan Galway didn't believe women belonged in the U.S.
Marines, but then a dangerous mission brought him and former marine pilot
Rhona McGregor together. Though he'd intended to ignore his beautiful copilot,
Nolan soon found himself wanting to surrender to the primitive hunger she
stirred in him....

#1460 THE SECRET BABY BOND—Cindy Gerard
Dynasties: The Connellys
Tara Connelly Paige was stunned when the husband she had thought dead
suddenly reappeared. Michael Paige was still devastatingly handsome, and
she was shaken by her desire for him—body and soul. He claimed he wanted to
be a real husband to her and a father to the son he hadn't known he had. But
could Tara learn to trust him again?

#1461 THE SHERIFF & THE AMNESIAC—Ryanne Corey
As soon as he'd seen her, Sheriff Tyler Cook had known Jenny Kyle was the
soul mate he'd searched for all his life. Her fiery beauty enchanted him, and
when an accident left her with amnesia, he brought her to his home. They soon
succumbed to the attraction smoldering between them, but Tyler wondered what
would happen once Jenny's memory returned....

#1462 PLAIN JANE MacALLISTER—Joan Elliott Pickart
The Baby Bet: The MacAllister Family
A trip home turned Mark Maxwell's life upside down, for he learned that
Emily MacAllister, the woman he'd always loved, had secretly borne him a
son. Hurt and angry, Mark nonetheless vowed to build a relationship with his
son. But his efforts brought him closer to Emily, and his passionate yearning for
her grew. Could they make peace and have their happily-ever-after?

#1463 EXPECTING BRAND'S BABY—Emilie Rose
Because of an inheritance clause, Toni Swenson had to have a baby. She
had a one-night stand with drop-dead-gorgeous cowboy Brand Lander, who
followed her home once he realized she might be carrying his child. When
Brand proposed a marriage of convenience, Toni accepted. And though their
marriage was supposed to be in-name-only, Brand's soul-stirring kisses soon had
Toni wanting the *real* thing....

#1464 THE TYCOON'S LADY—Katherine Garbera
The Bridal Bid
When lovely Angelica Leone fell into his lap at a bachelorette auction, wealthy
businessman Paul Sterling decided she would make the perfect corporate
girlfriend. They settled on a business arrangement of three dates. But Angelica
turned to flame in Paul's arms, and he found himself in danger—of losing his
heart!

SDCNM0802